BFF'S:

Best Frenemies Forever Series

Brenda Hampton

www.urbanbooks.net

Urban Books, LLC
97 N18th Street
Wyandanch, NY 11798

ISBN 13: 978-1-60162-402-4
ISBN 10: 1-60162-402-6

First Trade Paperback Printing February 2014
Printed in the United States of America

10 9 8 7 6 5 4 3 2

Distributed by Kensington Publishing Corp.
Submit Wholesale Orders to:
Kensington Publishing Corp.
C/O Penguin Group (USA) Inc.
Attention: Order Processing
405 Murray Hill Parkway
East Rutherford, NJ 07073-2316
Phone: 1-800-526-0275
Fax: 1-800-227-9604

Prologue

No words in the dictionary—not even the urban dictionary—could define how Cedric Thompson made me feel right about now. There was so much hatred in my heart for the man whom I used to love with ever fiber of my being. Surely, we'd had our ups and downs, highs and lows, but lately things had gone beyond anything I had ever imaged. He'd become disrespectful. He ignored my demands and how dare he try to sit back and call all of the shots. I tried my best to get him to see why we needed to be together, but he wasn't trying to hear me. He wanted everything to be his way, or no way at all. That was why the time had come for me to finally have it my way.

Thinking about this fucking disease he gave me, I glared straight ahead while driving my car in the direction of his house. My vision was blurred from tears in my water-filled eyes. The scars that he'd left cut deep; I was damaged beyond repair. For days, I pondered about what to do with the man who told me that he loved me and said that I meant everything in the world to him. Yet, when it came down to it, his actions didn't show what his mouth confessed. I was a fool to believe anything he'd said. The shame was on me for putting myself in this predicament. That in itself was hard for me to swallow, and so was the baseball-sized lump in my throat that was stuck there. As much as I swallowed, it wouldn't go away. The pain in my heart lingered, and the only satisfaction I would get was when Cedric Thompson lay dead in his grave.

With black leather gloves on, I squeezed the steering wheel tight. I could feel beads of sweat dot my forehead, and when I looked in the rearview mirror, my smudged mascara cascaded down my face with tears. Anger was trapped in my eyes. I was so upset that I growled loudly and slammed my foot harder on the pedal. I saw the speedometer needle jump from 60 to 90 mph as my car flew down the highway. My legs trembled from the crazy thoughts in my head, but I couldn't help but to crack a tiny smile when a vision of Cedric's dead body flashed before me. Needless to say, I was eager to get this over with. It was time. Time for him to answer for all the dirt he'd done, and go stand before his Maker. Oh, how I wished I could be there to hear his explanation for being such an asshole. He may have manipulated or gotten over on me, but there was no getting over on his Maker. Cedric would have to answer for his actions, and the punishment would be more brutal than the way I intended to do away with him.

My car rocked as I made my exit, rolling over a few bumps on the road. I decided to slow down, because the last thing I needed was for the police to come after me. I was so sure that I would be questioned after my beef was settled, but I had planned this day for many months. I already knew what to do, when to say it and how to say it. I suspected that no fingers would point to me, and with all of the trifling bitches in Cedric's life, finding the killer would be like searching for a needle in a hoestack. Or, at least, that was what I hoped. I hoped that this would be the end. That I would never have to look back on this day, feeling sorrow or having regrets.

Instead of parking my car in the curvy driveway, I parked down the street. My eyes searched the neighbors' houses that were close by Cedric's. I had to be sure that no one saw me. The darkness enabled me to hide the shotgun by my side, so I raced toward the front door with my heart slamming hard against my chest. A hoodie was thrown over my head, and the baggy jeans I sported barely hung onto my butt. My white tennis shoes were the only things that reflected in the night, but I wore them just in case I needed to run.

While at the door, I pulled a black mask over my face. With the leather gloves still on, I reached for the brass doorknob, turning it. The door *clicked* and opened immediately. I was surprised by the easy access, but rich people were always leaving their doors unlocked. Thing is, I had no idea where Cedric was inside. I had spoken to him today, and I'd seen him already too. All I knew was he was here. Somewhere inside. Unaware that he was minutes away from sucking in his last breath.

I tiptoed across the floor then step-by-step I climbed the carpeted staircase that led me to Cedric's bedroom. I expected to find him in bed, possibly rocking the shit out of it or asleep. But when I pushed on the double doors, they squeaked. The king-sized bed was empty and so was the rest of his bedroom. I inhaled the smell of his masculine cologne, then I went into his walk-in closet to look around. His tailored business suits, in almost every color, were neatly hung. His expensive leather shoes were stored in separate compartments and an island with drawers sat in the middle of the floor. On top of it were several expensive watches, gold cuff links, and diamond earrings that I assumed cost a fortune. I swiped up the items, stuffing them into my pockets. Since he had made me a homeless woman, I had to get something out of the deal.

I took a few steps away from the closet, causing the floor to squeak. That was when I heard Cedric's voice and realized that he was downstairs.

"Jacoby," he shouted. "Is that you?"

Of course, I didn't respond. I held my breath as I heard his hard footsteps on the stairs. While peeking through the cracked door, I observed as Cedric went into Jacoby's bedroom, looking for him. I suspected that Jacoby would be here soon, so I had to hurry and finish the job. Then, I needed to get the hell out of there.

I made another move and took a few more steps to get closer to the door. I could see Cedric coming my way, dressed in a silk robe. He reached inside to scratch above his dick, and when he pushed on the door, he was met with the barrel of my shotgun, aiming steady at his face. His eyes grew wide then they squinted as if he were trying to figure out who I was. That was kind of hard to do, because every inch of me was covered in black, with the exception of my tennis shoes.

"Wha— what do you want?" Cedric stuttered.

He carefully eased his hands in the air, keeping his eyes locked with mine. Fear was trapped in his eyes, and I was delighted to see the scared look he presented.

I held my finger on the trigger and Cedric's eyes shifted to it. "Please," he begged. "Don't do this. I'll give you anything you want. Wha—what is it that you want?"

I released my finger from the trigger and placed it over my red, glossy lips, signaling for him to hush. When my finger returned to the trigger, I took a few steps forward, causing him to step back. As I moved, he moved. He kept squinting and searching into my eyes, trying to figure out who I was. At this point, I didn't give a damn if he recognized me or not. We halted our steps at the top of the stairs, and that was when I signaled good-bye with a slow wink. His mouth opened, but before any words came out I lowered the shotgun to his buffed chest and happily squeezed the trigger.

The force from the gun jerked me backward, but I remained standing. I got much pleasure in watching

Cedric's body tumble down the stairs. His blood stained the clean carpet, and several of the rails broke loose as he tried to reach for them to break his fall. His body, however, landed on the cold, marble floor in the foyer. He lay there with his arms stretched wide, eyes gazing at the high ceiling. I moved slowly down the stairs, keeping a close watch on him as he gasped to catch his breath. Blood dripped from the corner of his dry mouth, and it also trickled from a deep scar on his forehead. I reached the bottom stair and stood over him with a wide smile that was visible behind the mask. His eyes fluttered, and wanting him to see who I was, I removed the mask and raked my fingers through my sweaty hair.

"Don't you know, Cedric? Too much pussy ain't good for you."

He strained to speak, but no words could be comprehended. His eyes fluttered a few more times before they shut and never opened again. His head tilted and the heaving of his chest came to a halt. I sucked in a deep breath then sighed from relief and grief. My mission was accomplished, or at least that was what I thought, until I saw someone staring at me through the glass front door. Right then I knew I was busted.

Chapter One

Evelyn

It had been a long day at work. I was completely exhausted. I breezed my Lincoln Navigator through the busy traffic in downtown St. Louis, trying to make my way home. My loft was on Washington Avenue. It was good to know that I was only ten minutes away from relaxation. My stomach was growling and my bed was calling me. I had worked overtime today so I could have extra money in my pockets to pay down the rising debt I found myself in. My girlfriends, Kayla and Trina, were the only ones who knew how messed up my financial situation was. But just so I didn't have to borrow any more money from them, I decided to pick up more hours at work. I also decided to do something else—something that I suspected my girls wouldn't approve of. That was find a man who could help me crawl out of my unfortunate situation. He was exactly what the doctor ordered. And there was no question that I had to give a little in order to get a whole lot. On-call pussy was what he wanted, but that didn't bother me one bit. I was willing and able to give him whatever, and for the past three months I realized how beneficial this relationship could be to me.

Minutes later, I entered the parking garage, parking my SUV into the reserved spot. That was the plus side of living in a loft apartment. I appreciated the privacy it offered. I used my swipe card to open the elevator that took me to my loft on the third floor. Dressed in a black pencil skirt and silver blouse, I sashayed down the narrow, carpeted hallway like a runway model. I had always wanted to be a model, and my slim figure had brought about many opportunities in the past. But then life happened. Moneywise, things didn't pan out for me. What I settled for was being a customer service representative, working for a white man who did nothing but boss our entire department around. It pained me to get up everyday and go to work, but I was blessed to have a job. Therefore, my complaints were kept to a minimum. I just had to put up with the bullshit until I could get the man in my life to save me by forking out more money.

I approached the bright red door to my loft with a smile plastered on my face; partially because I was home, but mainly because of the written note I saw taped to the door that instructed me to enter at my own risk. That meant Cedric was inside, waiting for me. I was delighted that he was there, only because we hadn't seen each other for almost two weeks. Our relationship was . . . complicated, but it was a relationship that I refused to tear myself away from.

I hurried to put the key in the door. The moment I walked inside, I was hit with the scent of Cedric's masculine cologne. A trail of pink and red rose petals were scattered on the hardwood, shiny floors. The petals made a path that led straight to my bedroom door. The door was closed and there was another note taped on it. I squinted behind my silver-framed glasses and still couldn't read the note. Eager to see what was up, I put my purse on the kitchen island and removed my high-heel pumps. My hair was parted through the middle and making sure everything was in order, I teased the flowing, blond-tinted tresses of curls with the tips of my fingers. I didn't have time to freshen my makeup, but with it being M·A·C, I was sure that it still looked fresh. My light, silky skin glowed from the shimmery lotion I wore. It didn't take much for me to present myself as sexy.

As I neared the door, the words on the note became clearer: *SOMETHING GOOD AWAITS YOU! HURRY!*

I rushed to open the door, feeling as if I had entered paradise. The strawberry-scented room was dim from the melting, flaming candles that burned on my nightstands. The trail of rose petals continued to the foot of the bed and a white sheet rested on the bottom half of Cedric's muscular frame. A smile was washed across his face, and as our eyes locked together in a trance, my heart started to race from excitement.

"What's up, sexy?" Cedric said, flashing his pearly-white teeth. "I hate to say it, but you know you looking more and more like my future wife, Evelyn Lozada, everyday. And not because of the first-name thing, baby, but because I said so."

My smile turned into a smirk as I started to undo my silky blouse. I pulled it away from my shoulders and began to create a pile behind me.

"I hate when you compare me to other women, and must I remind you that she doesn't have it like this." I flashed my goodies, hoping that Cedric appreciated what I was offering. "So, on another note, I'm glad you let yourself in. I'm highly interested in learning about the risk you mentioned at the front door, so why don't you tell me more about it?"

Cedric moved the sheet aside, exposing his flawless body that looked as if it had been dipped in creamy, milk chocolate. His dick stood at full attention, and as he relaxed sideways on his elbow, I walked to the bed and crawled my way up to him. Our eyes remained connected. When our lips finally touched, all I could do was shut my eyes and savor the taste of pure sweetness. My tongue danced with his, and like always, the lip-lock was intense.

Cedric held the sides of my face then backed away from me. "What did I ever do to deserve all of this?" he questioned.

"I could ask the same question, but I won't. I'll just say that we both should feel grateful and leave it there."

Cedric nodded then lay back on the bed. I straddled the top of him as he tucked a fluffy pillow behind his head and narrowed his light brown eyes to stare at me. His eyes scanned down my naked body. It didn't take much longer for his hands to roam. From the small curves in my hips to my plump ass that was just right, Cedric squeezed all of that and then some. I was so hungry for him that I reached for his package and positioned it to enter me. As my pussy lips sucked him into the heat I was packing, he closed his eyes. His hips started to grind in circles with mine, and the sound of my creamy juices being stirred played like theme music to our ears.

Minutes later, things sped up and we were going at it like two dogs in heat. The mattress squeaked and the loose headboard kept slamming against the wall. I was putting in some serious overtime, doing my best to please the one man who kept me satisfied more than any other.

"Yeah, you bad. Work that pussy on me, baby," Cedric said with a healthy portion of my ass gripped in his hands.

I rubbed the minimal hair on his buffed chest, and then gripped his broad shoulders so I could have something to hold on to when I increased my pace. I always got excited when he talked dirty to me, but there were times when he got too animated and went a little overboard.

"That's right, bitch!" he spewed through gritted teeth and smacked my ass. "Serve Daddy like you supposed to! Do that shit, girl, do it!"

By now sweat was raining down on my body. Per his request I was doing *it*. My pussy felt swollen from being beat by his mammoth-sized package that Cedric always used as a weapon. I was just about ready to cum. The moment my toes curled Cedric hurried to lay me on my back. He threw my long legs over his shoulders and broke into my insides like a thief in the night. For fifteen more minutes, we went at it. Then it happened: The same thing that happened every time we got together. It was always the one thing that brought our sex sessions to an end. I couldn't help myself from going there. I wanted to know what his wife had been up to, because I hadn't heard from her today.

"Why go there?" Cedric looked down at me with a blank expression on his face. "Why must you bring up her name every time we get together?"

"Because I can't help but to wonder how she would feel about all of this? I mean, do you fuck her as well as you screw me? I hate to keep asking, because one of you is lying. She says you do, you say you don't. What's really the truth?"

Cedric eased his dripping wet goodness from my insides, causing my coochie lips to lock. He released a deep sigh and shook his head.

"The truth is, all that shit you talking right now don't matter. I always try to do nice things for you, Evelyn, just so you'll recognize how much you really mean to me. You're pushing me away with your bullshit. Don't be mad at me when I tell you I've had enough."

As Cedric got dressed to go, I sat on the bed and pouted. Maybe I had been too hard on him, but then again, maybe not. After all, he was my friend's husband. Kayla would kill us if she knew about this, but this was not about me being in love with Cedric. I was in love with his money: Money that I needed right now and saw no other way to get it. Kayla had everything in life she wanted. Sharing a piece of her husband's dick wasn't going to cause her world to come tumbling down. She knew Cedric was no good, and after fifteen years of marriage all they did was put up with each other.

I honestly didn't view this situation as a big betrayal. I assumed that Cedric didn't love Kayla anymore and that she didn't love him. They stayed in their marriage because of their sixteen-year-old son, Jacoby. That in itself was the wrong reason.

Feeling kind of bad for bringing up Kayla around Cedric, I realized that I had some quick making up to do. But when I got out of bed, Cedric was dressed and ready to go. He was one fine man who knew how to turn up the heat in the bedroom. He also knew how to present himself as a professional businessman. The business suit he wore clung to his athletic frame that had been there since college. At thirty-eight, Cedric had his act together. I wasn't the only woman who craved him. Many people thought he was the real Columbus Short, and some women were foolish enough to run up to him for an autograph. So, not only did Kayla have her hands full with me, but she also had her hands full with tricks who desired to have her husband for his looks, and with those who wanted him for his money.

"I'm out," he said, glaring at me as I stood in front of him. He buttoned his suit jacket and backed away from me when I lifted my arms to place them on his shoulders.

"Evelyn, we're done for the night. Sex was good, but if you learn to keep your mouth shut you can always make it better."

He turned to walk away, but I followed him. "Forgive me," I said, knowing that he would. "I let the thoughts of Kayla get to me sometimes. I guess I shouldn't do that."

Cedric removed his keys from the living-room table then turned to face me. "I said it once and I'll say it again. Kayla is my concern, not yours."

"You're so right. From here on you will not hear me speak her name around you again. On another note, were you able—"

"Yes. The deposit is there. Check your account to be sure. If the money hasn't been deposited, let me know."

Cedric walked around me, making his way to the door. Knowing that the money was mostly likely in my account, the least I could do was send him off with a good-bye kiss. I hurried past him, just so he could get once last glimpse of my naked ass and come back for more. I reached for the doorknob to unlock the door, but Cedric stopped me when he inched close to me, pressing his body against my backside. He moved my hair away from my neck and planted a trail of soft kisses on it.

"I guess I'm forgiven," I said with a smile.

"Always," he whispered in my ear. "Especially since I can't resist that cute little dimple you have on your left ass cheek. Every time I see it, I just want to bow down and kiss it."

I wasn't sure if the dimple thingy was a compliment or not, but when Cedric squatted to kiss my ass I laughed. He laughed too then told me he needed to get going before he changed his mind about leaving.

"I'll call you tomorrow." He kissed my cheek and reached for the doorknob. I moved out of the way to let him exit.

"Tell Kayla I said hello."

Cedric glared at me then walked out. I watched as he smooth-walked his way to the elevator. Before it closed, I waved and he gave me a nod by tossing his head back.

Needing a shower, I closed the door and went into my bedroom. I turned my backside to the huge floor mirror that sat against my wall to check out the dimple on my ass. My ass and thighs were cellulite free, but Cedric was right. There was a dimple on my left cheek, and at thirty-six I didn't appreciate it. I frowned as I made my way to the bathroom to take a shower, but when I got out and checked my bank account, the money Cedric had deposited was there. That left a smile on my face. I wanted to call and thank him again, but instead I called Kayla.

"I'm in the middle of something," she whispered into the phone. "Can I call you back?"

I hoped that she wasn't in the middle of having sex. Just for the hell of it, I had to be sure. "You and Cedric are too horny for me. Why would you answer the phone during sex?"

"Uh, no. I'm at Jacoby's band concert. Don't you hear all the music in the background?"

"Oh, I do. Tell him that I'm sorry I couldn't make it. I'll make it next time. From what I can hear, though, the band sounds good. Is Cedric there too?"

"No. He hasn't made it yet. I'm not sure if he's coming. I don't care, either, but let me call you back, okay?"

"Sure. Sorry for interrupting. Don't forget to tell Jacoby what I said."

Kayla said she would and ended the call. I sat on the bed, thinking that if she didn't hold Cedric accountable for not being there for her and Jacoby, why should I care about all that was transpiring behind closed doors? As far as I knew, nobody suspected that anything was going on between Cedric and me. If he wasn't going to tell, neither would I. I was getting what I wanted; that was all that mattered. I swiped my hands together after I clicked the *send* button on my laptop to make my rental payment on time.

Chapter Two

Kayla

The school's auditorium was filled with plenty of parents, as well as grandparents and siblings, there to show support for the high school students in the jazz band. Jacoby had learned to play the saxophone years ago. His solo performance brought tears to my eyes. I sat proudly and my heart was filled with joy. There was a little disappointment too, as the chair next to me remained empty. Cedric said he would do his best to come, but I guess he couldn't pull himself away from his office chair that he was forever glued to. Either that or he could have been out somewhere wining and dining one of his tricks. I had a gut feeling that Cedric had been stepping out on our marriage, but after so many years together, some things weren't worth bringing to the kitchen table anymore. We had been there, done that before.

My main gripe was the relationship Cedric had with his son. Needless to say, I was disappointed. There was a time when the two of them were very close, but as Jacoby got older he started pulling away from Cedric. Jacoby barely wanted anything to do with him anymore, and they often walked around the house like two people who didn't know each other. I expressed my concerns to Cedric, but he blamed it on Jacoby's age. He said that as a growing teenager, Jacoby didn't want to be bothered and the two of us needed to back off and let him grow up. I agreed with that too, but there was much more to it that Cedric wasn't seeing. I figured it was up to Jacoby to tell him what was really going on with his attitude. I'd be lying if I said the way things were turning out didn't hurt.

The band instructor announced the last song of the night. That was when I looked up and saw Cedric walking down the stairs and making his way up to me. I wasn't sure if Jacoby saw him or not, but to be honest I was rather embarrassed by his late appearance. I crossed my legs, causing the slit in my ruffled yellow dress to slide over and show my cinnamon-brown skin. My metallic, pointed-toe heels matched my accessories, and my long, thin braids that flowed midway down my back were pulled away from my round face. My makeup was on like a work of art. The rich, plum lipstick I wore made me resemble Lauryn Hill, which was a plus because she was one of my favorite artists.

Cedric noticed me from all the brightness I added to the room. He displayed a forced smile before sitting next to me.

"You're late," I said with a little snap in my voice.

"Thanks for the announcement, but at least I'm here."

"Then maybe the standing ovation at the end of the concert should be for you. And by the way"—I turned my head toward him—"you should have showered before you came. The smell of sex can be calmed with hot water, you know."

Cedric held a smirk on his face and straightened his suit jacket. "And a loud mouth can always be silenced with a fist. Wrong place, wrong time, Kay. Silence yourself to prevent the embarrassment."

"You've already done that, and I welcome the idea of you putting your hands on me. You remember what happened last time you tried that mess. If I can recall, you lost a whole lot of sleep that night. Save your threats for that slimy hooker who didn't encourage you to wash up before you left her."

"Woman, would you shut up!"

The tone of Cedric's loud voice caused several people in front of us to turn around. It was a good thing that the band was louder than his voice, but I'd had enough. I got up from the seat I was in and went to sit in another one. I hated to carry on like this, but being around Cedric made me this way. There was a time when I loved him to death. I dropped out of college when I got pregnant with Jacoby. Shortly thereafter, Cedric and I got married. He finished college and jumped right into business with two other guys he'd met while in school. They all had computer science degrees that helped them create a profitable software development company that made them millionaires in less than five years.

Moneywise, we didn't have much to complain about, but everything else in our lives was a mess. The more money Cedric made, the more controlling, arrogant, and disrespectful he'd gotten. There were plenty of times that I wanted to leave him, but at this point I didn't have much to fall back on. I didn't want to start over and giving up all that I had didn't seem like the sensible thing to do. Then there was Jacoby. He was accustomed to the way we lived, even though he didn't always seem happy. He hated to hear Cedric and me arguing. I knew that the way we carried on was tearing him apart. That was why I did my best to hold my piece around him. The only time I confronted Cedric about my concerns was when Jacoby wasn't around. He still knew things weren't the best between his father and me, and the constant frowns on my face made my unhappiness quite clear.

The band was given a standing ovation after the concert was over. Cedric and I waited in the crowded hallway for Jacoby to put his instrument away and join us. Moments later he did. We both congratulated him on a job well done, and when he inquired about a critique of his solo performance, I quickly spoke up so Cedric didn't have to.

"It was awesome. Practice pays off and you are getting better by the day," I said.

Jacoby gave me a hug then he waited for a reply from Cedric. There was no doubt that he wanted his father's approval. For whatever reason, it meant more to Jacoby than my approval did. Cedric did what he knew best and lied.

"Yeah, that was the best I ever heard you play. Keep up the good work, son, I'm proud of you."

Cedric patted his back, but I suspected that Jacoby knew his father had only been there for ten minutes. Either way, we left the school together as a family. Jacoby and Cedric rode together in his Mercedes. I pulled off the parking lot in my black Jaguar. It was almost nine o'clock, but I figured Evelyn was still awake so I returned her call from earlier.

"Hello," she answered in a soft tone.

"Are you in bed already?"

"Yes, I am. I've been working a lot of overtime and I'm tired."

"I can understand that, but you've been sleeping a lot lately. You're not pregnant, are you?"

"Hell no, I'm not. I haven't had sex in almost a year. Besides that, you know I've had difficulties with getting pregnant."

"Well, you really need to take care of that D-thing because no woman your age should be without sex. I thought you were thinking about calling Marc again. He was real nice, Evelyn, and I don't think you gave him a fair chance."

"I did, but he failed the test. Nice, but broke. I'm already broke. The last thing I need is a broke man in my life."

"A rich man ain't all that, either, but you didn't hear that tad bit of information from me."

"Yes I did, and you, my sista, have no room to complain. Cedric is a for-real provider, and from what you say, he's pretty darn good in the bedroom too."

"That's fine and dandy, but his sexual capabilities don't matter right now. Do you know that he was late for Jacoby's concert tonight? And when he did get here, coochie was on his breath. Right after he sat next to me I could smell sex on him. Then again, maybe I'm saying these things because I'm upset about his tardiness. I don't know if he's been seeing other women or not, but it's hard for me to believe that he works late all the time."

Like always, Evelyn defended him. "Yeah, you need to stop exaggerating, Kayla. Cedric wouldn't dare come near you like that, and if he does have a little something on the side, so what. Any man who holds it down like he does should be allowed to do whatever he wishes. Instead of griping all the time, you need to be grateful that you're not in my situation—alone and broke. Let me know if you would like to trade places. I'm ready whenever you are."

"I'm not going to entertain your ridiculous comment about him being allowed to do whatever he wishes. The only reason I wouldn't trade places with you is because of my son. So, since we're on very different levels pertaining to this situation, I'm going to change the subject. Have you heard from Trina lately?"

"I spoke to her about two days ago. She just got back from an art show in New York. I'm surprised you haven't spoken to her."

"I've been busy. I'll call her tomorrow. Maybe we can meet for dinner, after church on Sunday."

"Who's cooking? You, me, Trina or Red Lobster?"

"The lobster sounds good, but I may be able to whip up something for us. I'll call to confirm before Sunday."

"Sounds good. Enjoy your evening and tell Cedric I said hello. Jacoby too."

"Will do. See you soon, Evelyn."

We ended our call, which left me in thought about my twenty-three-year friendship with Evelyn and Trina. Lord knows we all have had our ups and downs, but we remained very close. Sometimes, I questioned why because we didn't seem to have much in common. We didn't seem to understand each other at times. As we'd gotten older, the for-real support was lacking in every way possible. All we ever did was compete against each other, but when Cedric started bringing the money in, my whole life changed. I was able to afford the things that they couldn't. Where I lived—the Mansions at Williamson's Estates—couldn't even compare to the apartments they lived in. The cars I drove were very expensive, and while they shopped at the cheaper department stores, most of my clothes came from Saks or Neiman Marcus. I never thought that I was better than either of them, and even though I wasn't as happy as I should have been, I still viewed my life as a blessing. The plus side to our friendships was when I needed to vent, they were both there to listen. When my parents were killed in a car accident, I'll never forget how they stood by me. They were there when I had Jacoby, and since I had no siblings, it was good to have friends who I considered my sisters. Surely, things could be a little better between us, but maybe I was settling for so much BS because I feared having no one to turn to.

Minutes later, I entered the house and could hear Cedric and Jacoby arguing. I wasn't sure what it was about, until I walked into the kitchen and saw them standing face-to-face. Cedric had a smirk on his face, but Jacoby's forehead was lined with thick wrinkles. I had never seen him look so angry, so I rushed in between them to try and calm the situation.

"What is going on in here?" I asked with a twisted face.

"What's going on is your rotten-ass son wants to be the man of the house. He thinks he can speak to me any way he wishes and I'm not having that shit."

Jacoby fired back. "No, what's really going on is your husband is full of shit! I may as well be the man of the house, because in no way is he representing one."

"One more word, Jacoby, and I swear I'm going to knock you on your ass. No matter how you feel about me, I'm your father and you will respect me!"

"As your son, you need to respect me too. And if you feel a need to get some shit off your chest and knock me on my ass then do it!"

Cedric squeezed his fist, but I placed my hand against his chest. "Stop this," I shouted then looked at Jacoby. "Go to your room and cool out. I'll be in there to talk to you in a minute."

"Yeah, you better get him the fuck away from me," Cedric said. "Listen to your mother, son, she's a very wise woman."

Jacoby shook his head and walked away. "If she was wise, she would leave your sorry ass and find a better man. Unfortunately, Pop, you ain't him."

Cedric rushed around me and ran up to Jacoby. My heart dropped to my stomach when he tightened his fist and punched Jacoby in his face. Several inches taller than Cedric, Jacoby staggered backward, almost falling. When Cedric punched him in his stomach, that was when Jacoby doubled over and dropped to his knees. Cedric stood over him, pointing his finger near Jacoby's face.

"Talk like that will get you killed up in here. Consider this a warning."

Anger crept across my face as I saw Jacoby in pain. I rushed up and pushed Cedric away from him. "You didn't have to put your hands on him!" I shouted. "Can't you deal with your son without invoking violence?"

"No, I can't and if you put your hands on me again, wife or no wife, you're going to see more violence."

Like always, I had to remain the sensible one here, so I ignored Cedric. He stormed away, mumbling underneath his breath. I helped Jacoby off the floor, but he snatched away from me. He held his stomach and limped up the half-circle staircase to his bedroom. I hated to see my family go out like this, and I was anxious to find out what had happened between them in the car. With questions heavy on my mind, I made my way up the steps, but held on to the rail because I felt dizzy. Jacoby's room was next to the bonus room that was used for entertainment. His door was closed, so I knocked.

"Not right now, Mother," he said. "I'm not in the mood to talk."

"Get some rest and we'll talk tomorrow for sure. I thoroughly enjoyed your concert. Keep up the good work, okay?"

There was no response, so I moved away from his door with much sadness in my eyes. As I walked through the double doors to our master suite, I could hear water from the shower running. Cedric's clothes were in a pile on the floor, right next to our California king bed that was accessorized with mahogany and gold silk sheets. With throw pillows on top and with four thick columns surrounding the bed, it looked made for a king and queen. In front of the bed was a fireplace with a TV mounted above it. A small sitting room was to the left, and our humongous walk-in closets were to the right. There was a time when

I truly enjoyed being in this room with Cedric. Now, I hated it. I hated being in bed with him, wondering who he had been sharing another bed with. Our backs always faced each other's, and the last time we'd had sex was at least two, maybe three months ago. I could tell that things were getting worse by the day. After what had happened today, I wasn't sure how much more of this I could take.

By the time Cedric came out of the bathroom, I was already in bed with my nightgown on. My braids were tied down with a scarf. I had the remote control in my hand, flipping through the channels.

With a towel wrapped around his waist, Cedric went into his closet to hang his clothes. Minutes later, he got in bed and turned his back to me.

"Aren't you going to tell me what happened between you and Jacoby?" I inquired.

"Why should I tell you? You've already decided to take his side, so what happened between us doesn't really matter."

"I haven't taken anyone's side. All I said was that I didn't appreciate you putting your hands on him."

"And I don't appreciate you telling me how to be his father. You heard that insulting shit he said to me. If you think that it's okay for him to speak to me like that then you're just as fucked-up in the head as he is."

I put the remote down and glared at the back of Cedric's head. "If you want to be his father then you should have started your journey a long time ago. You can't wait until now to show up. He's not hearing you and he's definitely not down with you putting your hands on him at sixteen. Quite frankly, neither am I."

Cedric turned around and tossed the cover aside. "I refuse to stay in this room and listen to your bullshit about how I'm such a bad father. Yo' ass wasn't complaining when I bought that BMW for him last year, you weren't complaining when I paid for him to go to Italy with his classmates, nor were you complaining when I spent almost fifteen thousand dollars on a lavish sixteenth-birthday party that you wanted to have for him, just to impress your friends. Bad parents don't do that kind of shit, so get your facts straight first then we can talk on a level in which you need to be on."

Cedric headed to one of the guest rooms. I shouted out to him as he stomped down the hallway. "You can't buy his love, Cedric. It takes more than money to raise a child and he needs way more than that from you."

He stopped in his tracks, turning to look at me. "Since I have all of the money, why don't you step up your game through nurturing and guiding? After all, we are in this shit together, aren't we?"

I wanted to tell him to kiss my butt, but by then he had already closed the door. I seriously could not go on like this. Something had to change about this situation because I was starting to feel as if I were losing my mind up in here.

Chapter Three

Trina

The room was nearly pitch black, but I could see Lexi claw the sheets and suck in a deep breath. Her silky-smooth legs were wrapped around my neck and the sweet taste of her pussy always left me satisfied.

"More," she said in a soft whisper. "Then it's my turn to do you."

Giving her what she asked for—more—I slipped my tongue deeper into her hot pussy that covered my lips with a light glaze. Lexi rocked her lips against my mouth, and minutes later she expressed her excitement for me.

"I love you so much, Trina. No man has ever made me feel this way."

I knew exactly how Lexi had felt. Been there, done that, and what a waste of time it was. Day by day, I found myself being more attracted to women. I was even attracted to my girl, Evelyn, but if she and Kayla knew my situation they would never have anything to do with me. Even my own mother disowned me and so did my brother. I had no one but Kayla and Evelyn. They were considered my best friends. Still, there were some things I didn't want them to know. They often questioned me about why I rarely brought my male companions around, but to keep their concerns to a minimum I threw some of my male coworkers in the mix and introduced them to my girlfriends. From my coworker Keith to JaQuan, I toyed with them and made them believe I was interested. Truthfully, the only thing I was interested in was tasting more of Lexi and getting her to cum again before the night was over.

Almost an hour later, Lexi and I sat in a bathtub filled with bubbles. She was between my legs and the back of her head rested against my breasts. I lathered her body with soap, using my hands instead of a towel. While massaging her firm breasts, she squirmed around and tilted her head. I placed a trail of delicate kisses down her neck and lowered my hand to touch her stiff bud that peeked out of her coochie lips. Soft music played in the background and two glasses of wine sat on the edge of the tub.

"If you love me like you say you do," Lexi said, "why do you continue to keep our relationship a secret? I'm ready to tell the world how I feel about you. I'm a little disappointed that we've been seeing each other for almost two years and you don't acknowledge me as your woman."

Right then, I removed my finger from Lexi's insides. Sometimes, she griped a little too much for me. It was the wrong time to have this conversation that we had had over and over again. I hated to repeat myself and the last thing I wanted to do was hurt her feelings.

"I already told you why I didn't want to tell anyone about us. I have a lot to lose if I do. I thought you understood why I don't want to go there. My decision to stay quiet has nothing to do with how much I love you. I do, but I know the consequences behind me admitting our situation to others."

Lexi pouted, but then she took my hands, rubbing them together with hers. She remained quiet for a while, but minutes later she stood to get out of the tub. Suds rolled down her blemish-free body and her heart-shaped ass was so perfect that I couldn't allow her to leave. I rubbed up and down her long legs then I separated her ass cheeks as they faced me. She backed up and squatted so I could taste her again. With my fingers in motion too, Lexi shivered all over and cried out my name. We finished up our sex session in bed, and by morning she was on her way out.

Unfortunately for me, though, Lexi bumped right into Evelyn as she opened the door to leave.

Lexi's eyes widened. She searched Evelyn from head to toe. Evelyn peeked through the doorway with a smile plastered on her face. "Is Trina here?"

From in the kitchen, I waved my hand in the air. "I'm over here, Evelyn. Come right in."

Lexi moved aside to let Evelyn in. The look in Lexi's eyes said it all. She was jealous. She couldn't hide it. The twitching of her eyes alarmed me. I had to remind Lexi who Evelyn was so she wouldn't trip.

"Lexi, this is my best friend, Evelyn. Evelyn, this is my coworker, Lexi. She brought me some papers to sign this morning and joined me for breakfast. I guess you're here for breakfast too?"

They spoke to each other, but Evelyn quickly turned her attention to me.

"If you could cook," Evelyn teased, "I would love to join you for breakfast. But all you're going to offer me is cereal and milk, so no thanks."

"You got that right," I said, laughing. "But you're welcome to a bowl of Honey Nut Cheerios. We just had some, and the orange juice—if you want some—is back in the fridge."

Evelyn shook her head, signaling no. She then sat at the kitchen table. I moved toward the door with Lexi who appeared irritated by Evelyn's presence. After I opened the front door, we stepped outside of my apartment.

"So, what's up with you and this Evelyn chick?" Lexi
asked then folded her arms across her chest. "Are you
sure the two of you are just friends?"

Lexi had no reason to be jealous of Evelyn, because
she was just as pretty. The only thing with Lexi was her
attitude. At thirty-one, she was five years younger than I
was and she was a bit immature.

"I'm positive that the two of us are just friends. Now go
before you miss your spa appointment. I'll call you later."

Lexi rolled her big round eyes that were nearly hidden
behind her bangs. She tossed her straight, long hair to the
side and rushed off with much attitude on display. She
was a sexy biracial woman who stood about five feet two.
I was happy to have her in my life, but unfortunately, she
wasn't the only woman I was attracted to.

I tightened the belt on my sweatpants and pulled down
my tank shirt that cut right underneath my breasts. A
flowered tattoo flowed across my stomach and a belly
ring was clipped to my navel. I always wore my hair short
and layered, but it wasn't intact this morning. I hated that
it wasn't styled, only because I didn't like to be around
Evelyn when I didn't look my best. She was very critical,
unlike Kayla, who wasn't—especially not of me.

I went back inside, locking the door behind me. Evelyn
was on her cell phone talking to someone, but she rushed
to tell the caller she would have to call them back.

"What's up with that Lexi chick?" Evelyn questioned
then placed her phone on the table. "She had a real bad
attitude."

"She's always like that, so don't take it personal. The
people at work complain about her all the time and no
one really likes her."

I hated to lie, but I'd gotten pretty used to it. Evelyn
nibbled on her nails while looking around. "I like what
you've done to this place, but it's a little too colorful
in here. These bright yellow walls are working me. I

know you got this artistic stuff going on, but you should consider toning it down in here. I feel like I'm back in the seventies or something."

"I knew you would like my orange sectional and purple chairs, but how about you do you and let me do me? I'm sure you didn't come over here to talk about my weird paintings on the walls and how outdated my furniture is. What brings you by this early in the morning?"

Evelyn crossed her long, smooth legs, and then reached into her purse for a cigarette. After she lit it, she whistled smoke into the air and licked her perfect lips. "First of all, I stopped by to see you because I haven't seen you in a few weeks. I also wanted to find out if you were going to Kayla's house for dinner tomorrow. I've been trying to reach you all night, but your phone kept going to voice mail. I came here to check on you in person, just to make sure everything was okay."

I got up from the chair and went to check my phone. It was off the hook. With all the ruckus I caused with Lexi last night, we probably knocked the phone in my bedroom off the hook. I went to my bedroom, and sure enough the phone didn't have a dial tone. I put it back on the charger and then joined Evelyn again in the kitchen. I hated for her to smoke in my apartment. She kept fanning her hands in the air to clear the smoke.

"I don't have much else to do tomorrow, so I guess I will confirm with Kayla today that I'm coming to dinner. I assume she wants us to bring a dish, but whatever you do, please do not make any of that spaghetti you made the last time. That mess was awful."

Evelyn laughed and pursed her lips. "I made it taste bad on purpose. This time, though, I'm going to make a seven-layer salad and call it a day."

I looked up, pondering about what I had in the fridge to put together. Trying to see what, I got up and opened the stainless-steel door to the fridge.

"I . . . I guess I'll make a cheese tray with veggies. I may add some fruit to it too, unless I go to the grocery store and get something else."

"Uh, please do. I like to watch my weight, but my weekends are for splurging. Why don't you make lasagna? The last one you made was fire."

"I would love to make one, but do you see this figure I got?" I put my hands on my waist and twirled around. I was more fit than Evelyn and Kayla, only because I spent a lot of time at the gym working out. The muscles in my arms and abs were tight. "I don't want to ruin what I have going on with this body. When I weighed two-hundred-plus pounds in the eighth grade, you and Kayla couldn't stop teasing me. It took me years to get my weight under control, and lasagna is the last thing I need right now."

"Fine," Evelyn said, throwing her hand back at me. "Stick with the veggie tray and keep that muscle-packed, hourglass figure you got. You sure do have way more hips and ass than I do, but some men like all this slimness, so I'm good."

"Some men," I said, sitting back at the table. "Not all."

"Well, the one who matters does."

"Who may that be this month? And when are we going to meet him?"

"Maybe tomorrow. I may invite him to come with me tomorrow, so please be on your best behavior."

"I will, so no worries."

Evelyn and I sat for the next hour or so talking. I wasn't paying much attention to the conversation, because I was thinking that I didn't want to go to dinner tomorrow by myself. If I did, Evelyn and Kayla would surely question me about why I didn't bring a date. I kept thinking about who to call, Keith or JaQuan. I suspected that they were getting tired of playing this game with me. Both of them had been trying to get closer, but I wasn't having it. I pretended to be interested, but realistically, all they were good for was helping me keep up this front. The date thing wasn't the only thing on my mind. So was Evelyn. Sometimes, I felt uneasy in her presence, considering these crazy feelings I had. I felt terrible for eyeing her sexy lips as she spoke. When she got up to get something to drink, I admired her ass that was fitted into a stretch skirt. I wanted to see her naked—taste her and make love to her like I did Lexi last night. I'd had these feelings for a while—well, more so after I ended a bad relationship with my ex. It was so hard for me to keep this secret, but I had to. I couldn't tell Evelyn that all I wanted was one day with her. Just one. After that, I would want no more.

Evelyn stood and reached for her purse. "Well, it's been real, my friend, but I need to get to the cleaners to pick up my clothes. I wanted to go shopping today, but window shopping won't do."

"I agree. I'm down to my last hundred bucks. I just paid rent and the hundred dollars is all I have left until I get paid again."

Evelyn laughed. "At least you have that. I'm a broke bitch right now, but if I keep on working overtime it should help me get back on my feet. I don't want to borrow any more money from Kayla. I have yet to pay her back the two grand I already owe her."

"I know. I owe her twelve-hundred dollars and she told me to pay her back when I can. I was thinking about hitting her up for a few hundred tomorrow. I need something to help me make it to my next payday."

Evelyn and I let out a deep sigh at the same time. Our financial situations sucked, but I was thankful to Kayla for being there for us. She was a jewel. I really did appreciate our friendship.

After Evelyn left, I picked up the phone, trying to secure a date for tomorrow. Keith wasn't home so I called JaQuan.

"Did I catch you at a bad time?" I asked as I heard loud music in the background.

"No. I'm just stuck in traffic. There was an accident on the highway and nobody is moving."

"Sorry to hear that, but . . . uh . . . I have a question for you. Are you busy tomorrow?"

"Not really. Why? What's up?"

"I wanted to know if you would attend a dinner engagement with me. It's at my girlfriend's house and she invited me to come over."

"Which one of your girlfriends? The rich one or the snobby one?"

"The rich one. The one who is married to Cedric."

"I liked that dude. We had an interesting time at the baseball game that day and he seemed real down-to-earth. I wanted to talk to him about a business venture I'm interested in—so, yeah, I can do that. What time would you like for me to pick you up?"

"Around ten o'clock in the morning. If you don't mind, I'd like to go to church first. Then we can meet up with everyone for dinner."

"That's fine. See you tomorrow, Trina, and thanks for asking me to go with you. You must be my good-luck charm because traffic is finally moving again. Way to go, huh?"

"Yeah. See you soon, JaQuan. Be safe."

The next morning, JaQuan was right on time picking me up. He complimented the brown dress I wore that melted on my curves like a chocolate candy bar. My hair was layered and the makeup I wore dolled-up toffee-colored skin. The gold strappy heels I wore gave me much height; I was almost as tall as JaQuan, who stood almost six feet two. He was a head-turner too. What woman didn't appreciate a light-skinned man with confidence? He defined sexy. His facial hair was neatly trimmed and his haircut was sharply lined and cut into a fade with waves. He wasn't what I would call muscle-packed, but the man did have a fit body. Too bad it didn't do much for me. The good thing was that being around JaQuan was fun, because he was very comical.

We arrived fifteen minutes late for church, but were lucky enough to find seats that provided a clear view of the pulpit. Pastor Clemons sat in his chair, watching as church folks filled the sanctuary from the first pew to the back. The announcements were being read, and a few minutes later the ushers began to take an offering. When the choir started to sing, several people stood, clapping their hands. The first lady, Cynthia, was always there to show her support. Even though her husband was the biggest player in the church, she stood by him. But the truth was, she wasn't on the up-and-up, either. She had flaws, like many of us who were there to cleanse our souls.

After the choir finished singing, Pastor Clemons approached the podium.

"Amen," he shouted.

"Amen!" the congregation shouted back.

"We have one of the best choirs in St. Louis. Don't forget to get your tickets for the annual concert. When I tell y'all this choir is going to set the roof on fire, I mean it!"

The congregation laughed and clapped their hands. My eyes were focused on Cynthia, who kept turning her head to the side, looking at me. I could see her staring, but I ignored her. JaQuan seemed to pick up on the constant eye gestures, and it didn't surprise me when he leaned in to inquire about Cynthia's actions.

I shrugged my shoulders. "I'm not sure. It looks like she's checking you out."

Of course, she wasn't. Because, like me, the first lady loved women and got excited whenever she saw me. She knew what I was capable of doing to her, and it had been almost a month since we'd had one of our sexual escapades. Cynthia told me that she wanted to call it quits because Pastor Clemons was starting to get suspicious. The last thing she wanted was to lose her status as the first lady. According to her, there were plenty of women waiting to take her place.

No matter what, though, I didn't attend church to see her. I didn't come to judge anyone. I was there to save myself. I knew the way I was living my life wasn't right, and I looked forward to asking God to forgive me, especially on Sunday mornings.

Church let out a few hours later. JaQuan left me standing on the stairs while he went to get the car. That was when Cynthia took the opportunity to approach me.

"Hey there, Sister Watson," she said while holding on to her wide-brim hat that was about to blow off her head. The sun was shining bright, but the wind was gusty. I leaned in to give her a hug and she hurried to whisper in my ear. "I need to see you. Can I stop by tonight?"

I backed away from her, forcing a fake smile. "I'll call you on Wednesday. Maybe we can get together for Bible study. Until then, give Pastor Clemons my love."

I moved quickly down the concrete steps, making my way to the car. Luckily, several other members of the church crowded around the first lady to talk. That way she couldn't come after me. I was glad about that. JaQuan already had a bunch of suspicion in his eyes. The last thing I needed was for him to dig deeper into what was really going on between me and the first lady at Stone Mount Baptist Church.

Chapter Four

Evelyn

To be honest, I was not looking forward to dinner at Kayla's house, but what the hell? I didn't want her to suspect anything between me and Cedric. The best thing I could do was show up with a man and pretend that he was my lover, instead of her husband. I hadn't spoken to Cedric since the other day, but like Trina, I was also low on cash. After rent was taken care of, that didn't leave me with any money to play with. I needed something in my pockets, especially since I saw these Jimmy Choo shoes I wanted yesterday while browsing the mall. Having nothing else to do yesterday, I went ahead and drove to the mall. I wished Trina had gone with me. It seemed as if she needed to get out and have some fun. But when you're broke, getting out and doing things was hard to do. I definitely knew where she was coming from, and I looked forward to the day when the two of us would get out of the ruts we were in.

Marc, the poor excuse of a man I elected to take with me as a date, said his car was in the shop, so I went to his house to pick him up. We had dated several years ago and still kept in touch. We made great phone buddies, but a relationship we could never have again. We couldn't seem to click and we argued more than anything. The only time we got together was when he needed to show-case me around his family and friends. I used him for the same reasons, so he wasn't too enthused when I called and invited him to attend dinner with me. There wasn't a chance in hell that I was going to this dinner alone. I had to show Cedric that I wasn't as hooked on him as he thought I was. I was hooked on his money more than anything, and maybe—just maybe—a little hooked on his sex too.

Marc had been running his mouth the whole time in the car. He looked decent in his jeans and polo shirt, but the smell of his breath was tearing up my nostrils. His bald head had a shine to it and his tinted sunglasses covered his hazelnut-colored eyes. His body was sculptured like a linebacker, and my only other complaint was his dingy tennis shoes that needed to be washed with Tide.

"Am I allowed to kiss you while we're here?" he asked as I was only five minutes away from Kayla's and Cedric's house.

"No, you're not. Do not hug or touch me, either. Just be friendly and say nice things about me."

"Now, that's going to be hard for me to do," he said with a smile. "I don't know too many nice things about you, so you may have to help me out with this."

I rolled my eyes, even though I figured Marc was joking around. A few minutes later, I pulled into the arched driveway in front of their two-story brick house. The bay windows were sparkling clean, the bushes were neatly trimmed, and beautiful tulips were starting to bloom. The grass was well manicured and the outside of their home looked fit for the cover of *Better Homes and Gardens* magazine. Three other cars were already there, but I wasn't sure who they belonged to. Before we exited the car, I reached in my purse to offer Marc a stick of gum.

"Thank you," he said, reaching for it. "I was going to ask if you had any gum. You must have read my mind."

Good thing he couldn't read mine. All I did was smile and check my beautifulness in the rearview mirror. The curls in my hair were working for me, my makeup was done to perfection, and the summer orange skirt I wore matched my thong sandals. My white sleeveless tank stretched across my breasts and a simple gold necklace I wore matched my hoop earrings. I felt great about my appearance, even though Marc had failed to acknowledge how spectacular I looked. That was another thing that I hated about him. He was so into himself that he didn't have anything good to say about anyone else. I could only laugh to myself. I guess the same could be said about me.

With the seven-layer salad in my hands, I rang the doorbell and looked through the double glass doors that viewed the loveliness of the house. The marble-topped foyer could be seen, as well as a hanging chandelier. I saw Jacoby walking down the circular staircase and then Kayla appeared with a welcoming smile on her face. As she opened the door, I checked her out. She had on a white linen jumpsuit, accessorized with silver jewelry. Her long braids were pulled away from her face and I couldn't deny that she had the prettiest round eyes I had ever seen. She was such a classy lady and her sweet perfume smelled a whole lot better than Marc's breath. I leaned in to air kiss her cheeks then I thanked her for inviting us.

"You remember Marc, don't you?" I said, looking at his lust-filled eyes that were glued to Kayla.

Marc reached for Kayla's hand, kissing the back of it. "Of course she remembers me. Hello, beautiful," he said.

Kayla blushed, but pulled her hand away from him. "Hi there, Marc. Come on back to the kitchen. We should be ready to eat in about another hour or so. Please make yourselves at home."

How I wished I could make this my home. Kayla had it made, yet she seemed so ungrateful. I never understood why she always seemed so unhappy, either. If I had it like this, all of my problems and worries would be solved. In addition to that, she had a good-looking man to wake up to every morning. Not a man in off-brand tennis shoes that were dirty like Marc's were.

Either way, we followed Kayla into the immaculate kitchen that was every woman's dream come true. A granite-topped island sat in the middle of the floor and the hardwood floors had a shine that showed my reflection. An apple pie was baking in the double oven, along with rotisserie chicken that I couldn't wait to tear into. Another salad was already on top of the island and so were an array of desserts, vegetables, pastas, and fruit.

Trina sat at the oval-shaped table next to a man who I had seen her with twice before. He was rather cute to me. I preferred to have him as my date than Marc. Cedric looked spectacular in his cargo shorts, Nike shirt, and cap. He looked up to speak then lowered his head to read the golf magazine that was on his lap. Trina introduced me to JaQuan, and then she got up to acknowledge me. I placed the salad on the island before I embraced her.

"Good seeing you again," she said. "I hope that salad you made is better than the one Kayla made."

"I doubt it," Kayla said.

"We'll just have to see about that, won't me?" I shot back, but was serious about my salad tasting much better than hers.

We laughed and walked over to the table to sit. The only person who hadn't joined us was Jacoby. He spoke to us in a dry tone then headed back upstairs.

I looked across the table at Kayla, who was sitting next to Cedric. "What's wrong with Jacoby? I've never seen him look so glum. Is that a bruise on the side of his face?"

Kayla and Cedric looked at each other. After rolling her eyes at him, she quickly spoke up.

"Jacoby and one of his so-called friends were wrestling and he got punched. Besides that, he's a sixteen-year-old with a chip on his shoulder."

"No, he's a sixteen-year-old who needs to get his shit together," Cedric added. "That's what his problem is."

No one at the table bought that bullshit. It was obvious that Cedric was responsible for the mark on Jacoby's face, but I wasn't going to question why Cedric wasn't getting along with his disrespectful son. That was their business.

The men at the table started a heated conversation about how the young men were conducting themselves these days. I didn't have much to add because I had no children and I didn't plan on having any, either. For whatever reason, Kayla didn't appreciate where the conversation was going. She kept rolling her eyes and sighing every time Cedric said something.

"Can we please change the subject?" she suggested. "I can tell you why I think many of the young men out there act the way they do, but I don't want to hurt anyone's feelings."

I could sense something between her and Cedric. Just to spark up a heated conversation between them, I encouraged Kayla to speak up when I added my two cents.

"I mean, I think it has a lot to do with these boys being fatherless," I said. "And some of the absent fathers need to take responsibility."

"I agree," Kayla said. "And some have fathers who don't know how to be fathers. It's a mess. I'm just doing the best that I can with Jacoby."

"Yeah, *we* are," Cedric said, correcting her. "I hear what both of y'all are saying, but there are some lazy women out there half-ass raising boys too. And when the men try to step up, they got issues with it. I think it's wrong to put the blame solely on the men, especially when some mothers need to get their shit together."

Of course the other men agreed, but I knew that Marc had no room to talk. He wasn't even paying child support. All he did was gripe about his son's mother begging for money, so he needed to shut the fuck up. Cedric was holding his family down, but I didn't necessarily see that father-and-son connection between him and Jacoby. And based on what Kayla had said, Cedric was slacking. I wasn't sure what was up with JaQuan, but maybe I would get to know a little more about him after dinner was over.

Trina and I got up to help Kayla in the kitchen. The men continued their conversation, but every now and then Cedric and I kept taking peeks at each other. I hoped we weren't being too obvious, but I wondered if he had those naughty thoughts swarming around in his head like I'd had. Needing some extra cash, I had to figure out a way to get him away from everyone before I left.

Dinner was ready and we all circled the island, holding hands. Trina blessed the food and everyone got a plate to pile it with food. Cedric filled our flute glasses with wine and Kayla made sure that we all had everything we needed. She was such a good host and she was at the top of her game when it came to being organized. Jacoby didn't join us, but as soon as we all sat at the table to eat, he came into the room with the same long look on his face.

"Do you mind if I go over to Adrianne's house?" he asked Kayla.

"I don't care, Jacoby. Only for a few hours."

Jacoby nodded and then turned to walk away. That was when Cedric spoke up. "She said only for a few hours. That doesn't mean you need to stroll up in here at midnight. If you do, you're going to find yourself on punishment."

Jacoby shrugged. "There is no reason for you to be co-signing, because I heard what she said. If I'm going to be late, like always, I'll call."

Cedric wasn't backing down. "If you heard what she said then that means don't be late. If you are, a punishment will be enforced. Period. End of discussion."

"Whatever. I'm out."

Cedric didn't appreciate his tone, and quite frankly, neither did I. He was about to get out of his chair, but Kayla reached for his arm. "Would you please stay seated and let him get out of here? I'm trying to enjoy dinner with my guests, and I don't have time to entertain a dispute between you and Jacoby."

Cedric snatched his arm away from Kayla and got up anyway. She didn't have enough power to tell that man what to do, and it was so apparent that he was the one in charge around here.

"Jacoby," Cedric shouted after him, halting his steps. "Don't you *whatever* me. You'd better listen to me when I speak. Understand?"

Jacoby's whole face was twisted. He didn't say another word, but the look in his eyes showed much hatred for his father.

"As I was saying," Cedric continued. "Since you got an attitude, you don't need to go anywhere right now. Go chill out in your room and think about how you need to get at me."

We all watched, holding our breaths. Kayla was so embarrassed that she dropped her napkin on the table and got up to go intervene. "Just let him get out of here, Cedric. We have guests right now and this is seriously the wrong time."

"Wrong time," Cedric said. "Maybe so. I'd hate for anyone to see me beat that ass, and just so you know, you're never too old for me to do it. Now, get the hell out of here before I change my mind."

Jacoby didn't flinch. He released a light snicker and walked away. Kayla and Cedric returned to the table, and it was obvious that things were very heated around here. Everyone's eyes shifted around the table and we were quite speechless. I was a little relieved when JaQuan spoke up and changed the subject.

"Well, on a more positive note, Trina and I are getting married," he said.

All heads snapped in his direction. Trina's jaw was dropped and her mouth was wide open. "What?" she shouted. "Uh, I don't think so. Where did that breaking news come from?"

JaQuan laughed and sipped from his glass of wine. "Calm down," he said, laughing. "I'm just kidding. Thought I'd say something that would get us off that rocky path and on to another one."

Trina didn't find any humor in what JaQuan had said. She turned to him and got to the point. "I didn't find your little joke funny. Next time, I would appreciate if you wouldn't include me in it."

JaQuan shrugged his shoulders and didn't seem to trip. I didn't know what was going on, but this setting wasn't working for me. I was so glad that Marc had kept his mouth shut, but I guess my thoughts were too soon.

"Kayla, I must admit," he said, "the food is dynamite and you truly outdid yourself. You're going to have to invite me over here more often, or I need to invite you to my crib so you can come cook for me."

I dropped my fork. His comment was very disrespectful and all Cedric did was stare at him from across the table. Kayla blushed, obviously loving the attention. "Thank you, Marc. I will invite you over again—and wait until you taste my meat loaf. I'll cook that next time."

He was all smiles and had the audacity to lick his lips. "That's what's up. I would love to come over here again. And FYI, I cook too. Maybe I can show you a few of my good recipes and you can hook me up in return."

"Sounds good to me. I love it when people hook me up."

They laughed, but neither I nor Cedric heard shit funny. He cocked his head back, looking at Kayla's ol' disrespectful ass. "Hook you up? Really? Well, before you hook him up, you need to hook me up. Hook me up with some daily meals, some back rubs, and with some pussy. Can you handle that for me, Mrs. Wifey?"

Before Kayla could respond, Cedric looked across the table at Marc, who had paused from eating his food. "This dinner will probably be over with real soon. Until then, watch what you say to my wife. I don't appreciate the disrespect and the fact is, she won't be hooking you up, nor will you be hooking her up with shit. No one comes here unless I invite them . . . so it doesn't look like you'll be visiting us anytime in the near future."

I was a little jealous about Cedric's "wife" comment. Did he really care? Maybe he was jealous, but why? Marc was very out of line. He couldn't compete with Cedric, and I always admired how Cedric handled himself. Listening to him put Marc in his place made my pussy wet. He'd have to take care of that little problem for me real soon.

"I didn't mean any disrespect," Marc said. "I was just complimenting her food. It's been a long time since I had a meal like this one, and the women I've dated can't touch this. Her cooking makes me feel like I'm at home . . . like when I'm at my mother's house. That's all I was saying and it wasn't about me trying to hook her up with anything else."

"Thank you for clearing that up, Marc," Kayla said, rolling her eyes. "I don't know why anyone would assume we were talking about anything other than food."

She played clueless, but Cedric and I knew better. Marc did as well. I felt as if the stanky-breath fool insulted me. I knew where he was going with his comment about not having a good meal, and it was his way of not saying anything nice about me as I had asked.

"It's a good thing that we never got around to dating each other," I said. "Because had we done so, you would know that I can cook my butt off. I do so at times, especially for the men who mean a lot to me."

I couldn't help but to look at Cedric, referring to how well I cooked for him. Right then, though, I felt someone's foot rub against my leg. I thought it was Cedric's foot, but he had an irritated look locked on his face like he was so done with this dinner. My eyes shifted from one person to the next. Trina was the only one looking at me. I blinked fast and the foot rubbing stopped.

"Is that you?" she questioned. "I thought you were JaQuan. Forgive me."

Everyone looked at us, not knowing what was going on. My leg didn't feel like JaQuan's. Trina needed to correct herself, because she was about to get cussed out for rubbing her feet on me. I got back to my food, admitting to myself that everything was delicious. JaQuan and Trina raved about the food, but the last thing Kayla needed was for me to swell her head even more. She definitely wouldn't get any praise from me.

The next hour was filled with jabs, conversation, and laughter. Once dinner was done, the men headed downstairs to the entertainment room to play pool while me, Trina, and Kayla stayed in the kitchen to clean up. I couldn't help but to ask Kayla what was going on between her and Cedric. Whatever was going on she pretended like everything was all good.

"We're just a married couple who have minor issues that can be worked out. It's really nothing, but I'm hoping that him and Jacoby reconcile their differences soon."

"I hope so too," Trina said. "It seemed like things were about to turn ugly."

Kayla refused to go any further. She continued to stack the dishes in the dishwasher while I packed up the leftovers and put them in the fridge. Trina cleared the table and wiped it down, along with the countertops.

After the kitchen was spotless, we joined the men downstairs. I kept thinking of a way to get Cedric alone, but he seemed immersed with shooting pool.

For the time being, I sat on the leather sectional and watched a reality TV program with Trina and Kayla. We couldn't stop talking about how ridiculous the women were, but to be honest, the reality shit was going on right in this room.

Cedric must've read my mind when he told Kayla he was going upstairs to return a business phone call. I saw it as the perfect opportunity for me to step away, and while Marc and JaQuan started another game of pool, and Trina and Kayla's eyes were glued to the TV, I announced my departure.

"I'm going outside to smoke." I knew Kayla wouldn't allow me to smoke in her house. "I'll be right back."

"Hurry, because I'm not going to rewind this until it's over," Kayla said. "You're going to miss the new chick getting slapped. I think it's coming up next."

"I'm sure y'all will tell me all about it when I get back."

They assured me that they would.

I made my way upstairs to find Cedric. The moment I reached the top stair, he was standing by the kitchen counter, waiting. He placed one finger over his lips, as a gesture for me to be quiet. He then nudged his head toward the garage door and walked toward it. I followed. Inside of the five-car garage was a fleet of lavish cars that belonged to him and Kayla. The only spot that was empty was the spot where Jacoby parked his car. Cedric unlocked the car and he opened the back door to his Rolls-Royce that provided plenty of room in the backseat.

"Are you serious?" I whispered to him. "We're just going to talk, aren't we?"

"Ay, that's all I want to do, unless you have something else in mind like *hooking me up*."

We laughed and I got in the backseat with him. Talking wasn't in our plans. His hands eased up my skirt, and the moment his fingers slipped into my wetness, I turned on my stomach. Cedric unzipped his pants and flipped up the back of my skirt. He moved my thong to the side and filled my hot pocket with his hard, thick meat that always guaranteed me an orgasm.

"You know I'm jealous," Cedric whispered in my ear while long stroking me from behind. My ass was hiked up and the sounds of my pussy juices made him aware that he was hitting the right spot.

"Jealous of who or *whaaaat*?" I moaned. "You have *noooo* reason to be jealous. I'm the one who is jealous. Jealous of Kayla for getting a piece of this whenever she wants to."

"You can have a piece whenever you want to. Just ask for it. And the next time you come over here, leave the broke-looking joker at home. He's an embarrassment and I know you can do much better."

"I can. That's why I'm doing it with you and not with him."

Cedric tore into my insides and rushed me to the finish line so we could hurry to go back inside. The car rocked fast from the speed of our action, but as soon as I opened my mouth to react to him busting my cherry, the garage door lifted. Cedric covered my mouth with his hand and we dropped low on the floor in the backseat. My pussy was dripping wet from a mixture of our juices, and the feel of Cedric's dick still in me felt spectacular.

For whatever reason, I was hoping that Kayla would see us. It wasn't that I hated her or anything like that. I had just lost a lot of respect for an ungrateful bitch who didn't realize or appreciate what she had. Cedric peeked through the tinted windows and whispered to me that it was Jacoby, not Kayla. He waited until Jacoby was inside before he hit me with a few more strokes that tickled my insides and gave me something more to smile about. He had definitely gotten what he wanted, but now it was time for me to get what I wanted.

"Before we go back inside, I need to ask you for a favor. I know you're getting tired of me, but until I find another job, I don't—"

"How much," Cedric said then planted a kiss on my cheek.

"Several hundred dollars. Whatever you can spare is fine with me. Anything will help me right about now."

"I'll transfer the money into your account in the morning. And don't be ashamed to ask me for money. We have to look out for each other."

No doubt we did. I was very appreciative of Cedric's generosity. Like always, he came through for me and I intended to always come through for him.

Ten minutes later, Cedric and I entered the house as if nothing had gone on between us. We returned to the basement together, telling Kayla and Trina that he took me to his office to show me his collection of autographed baseballs he had from several St. Louis Cardinals players.

"Evelyn didn't believe how much my balls were worth," Cedric said. "I had to prove to her, as well as show her that they were worth a lot."

His balls were definitely worth a lot—to me they were. I was on a serious high from what had transpired, but when I checked my account the next morning, I was pissed. Cedric had only deposited a hundred dollars, when I clearly said *several* hundred were needed. I called to chew him out, but unfortunately for me his voice mail came on. Cheap bastard. I thought . . . oh, no, he didn't. I checked my account again, realizing . . . oh, yes, he did.

Chapter Five

Kayla

These ongoing arguments between me and Cedric were getting on my nerves. They were embarrassing and we were starting to lose too much respect for each other. I wanted to calm things down and see if we could somehow start working on our marriage that was falling apart. I knew that Cedric would never agree to counseling, but we had to do something to get our lives back on track. Jacoby was being affected by this. I couldn't sit by much longer and watch our family being torn apart.

Cedric was at work, so I decided to take him lunch so we could talk. I wasn't sure how late he was working tonight, and I was ready to get some of my concerns off my chest. When I arrived at his office, dressed in a long, multicolored sundress and sandals, the bubbly receptionist directed me to go ahead on back to his office.

"He should be in there," she said, checking me out from head to toe. She also looked envious of me, but she didn't have to worry about me being envious of her. She was a trashy-looking white chick who one of Cedric's partners had offered the position to. I wasn't sure if Cedric's partner, John, was involved with her or not, but he did have a wife who I knew very well.

As I approached the door to Cedric's office, I could hear him speaking to someone over the phone. He spoke in a light whisper, but busted into a fit of laughter a few times.

I heard him refer to the caller as "sweetheart" and not knowing if he was flirting or not, I entered his office with a forced smile on my face. He was leaned back in his chair with the phone up to his ear. The noticeable hump in his pants surprised me and the smile on his face vanished.

He slowly sat up, clearing his throat. "Uh, let me call you back later. I need to take care of something right now."

Not waiting for a response, Cedric put the phone down and looked at the bags in my hand.

"I thought you might want some lunch," I said. "But if you're busy, I can always come back."

"Nah, I'm good. That was just someone I'm trying desperately to close a business deal with. Have a seat and thanks for thinking of me."

"I always think of you, Cedric. Whether you know it or not."

I sat in the chair in front of his desk and opened one of the bags. I pulled out a turkey sandwich, some chips, an apple, and a diet Coke. I baked some chocolate chip cookies too, so I laid those on the desk as well.

"I feel like a school kid," he said with a smile. "Please tell me what I did to deserve this, Mom?"

"Sarcasm will get you nowhere with me. Now eat up and let's talk about what has been going on with our marriage."

Cedric bit into the apple and leaned back in his chair. He gazed at me from across his desk, narrowing his eyes. "You look nice," he complimented. "But as far as our marriage goes, what about it?"

"I can't believe you have to ask." I opened my can of diet Coke and took a sip. "We've been arguing day in and out. I don't think you're happy anymore, and I'm here to ask if you want a divorce."

Cedric sat silent for a few seconds. He bit into the apple again and chewed. "No, I don't want a divorce. I admit to not being completely happy, but you're not happy, either."

"No, I'm not. We really need to do something about this because I don't like how we're treating each other. I'm willing to do whatever I must do to correct our problems, but you need to tell me what it is that you need from me. Then I'll share what I need from you. We have to work at improving on the things that are hindering us from growing together in a respectful and healthy marriage."

"I would love to talk about all of that, but why talk about it here? You know that I have work to do, Kay. We'll have to discuss this when I get home."

"That's fine, only if you're coming home at a decent hour. Are you working late tonight?"

"As of right now I'm not. But I'll do my best to be there by seven."

"Seven o'clock is fine. That way I'll have time to talk to Jacoby before you get there and see if he'll go hang out with his friends tonight so we can have some privacy."

"Sounds like a plan."

Cedric and I ate lunch together in peace. Before I left, he gave me a peck on the lips and patted my ass as I walked out the door. He didn't know that I had an earful for him tonight. Maybe it was a good thing that we didn't have our conversation on his job, because I expected things to get heated.

When I arrived home, I waited for Jacoby while watching TV in the family room. He was late, and when I called his cell phone he told me that he stayed after school.

"After I get done with band practice, do you mind if I go to Adrianne's house for dinner? Her mother invited me to come over and then we want to go to the mall. I promise not to stay out late, and I'll have my cell phone available if you need to reach me."

"I don't mind. Have a good time and tell Adrianne's mother I said hello."

"I will."

I sat on the couch thinking about Jacoby. He was a good kid. Any bad behavior that he had been representing was due to what was transpiring at home. He had a look in his eyes like he hated his father. I was going to do my best to change things around.

By seven o'clock, Cedric wasn't there. He finally came home close to eight. I waited for him to eat dinner then he joined me in the family room. Still dressed in his suit, he sat on the couch next to me and wiped his mouth with a napkin.

"Okay, Kay, tell me what's on your mind."

"I plan to, but I would like to start with you telling me what you expect or want from me. I assume I'm making some mistakes. I don't know what they are unless you tell me."

Cedric's cell phone rang and he pulled it from his pocket to see who it was. He winced then slipped the phone back into his pocket. "For the most part, my only problem with you is how you interfere in my relationship with Jacoby. I don't appreciate how you take his side all the time, and for so many years you have tried to tell me how to be a father. That's an insult to me. I don't need your assistance and your behavior has caused me to put up a wall between me and my son. I'm real pissed about it too. What I need for you to do is back off and support me sometimes."

"I can do that, okay. I do understand where you're coming from and I have made some mistakes pertaining to that. Forgive me for not being supportive. I hope it's not too late for the two of you to fix things."

Cedric shrugged. "We'll see. I was thinking about asking him to join me next weekend on a business trip so we can talk. Just me and him, without you."

"That's fine with me. I'm sure I can find something to do while the two of you are away."

"I'm sure you can too, but whatever you do, please don't invite Marc over here to feed him. Don't invite Trina over here, either."

My brows shot up. I was surprised to hear Cedric say that about her. "Why wouldn't I invite Trina over here? She's my best friend and she is always welcome into my home."

"She should be welcomed, but not when I'm not here. I prefer to keep my eyes on her, if you know what I mean."

"No, I don't know what you mean. Please explain yourself to me, because I don't know why you feel a need to keep your eyes on Trina."

Cedric stood and stretched. "Baby, come on. You've been knowing Trina for many, many years. Don't sit there and tell me that you don't know she's gay."

My eyes bugged and mouth opened wide. "What? Have you lost your doggone mind? Trina is far from being gay. Why would you say that about her?"

"Because I know a gay woman when I see one. Like always, she didn't have no connection with her date and they barely talked to each other. They didn't even touch and he was almost like some kind of prop for her. In addition to that, I've never seen her checking me out. Whenever a woman doesn't look at me, I know something is wrong with her."

I pursed my lips and threw my hand back at him. "If you think Trina is gay because she doesn't look at you, you're a fool. She doesn't show interest because you just happen to be married to her best friend. Stop being so arrogant and full of yourself, Cedric. Some women may not find you attractive, and I've never heard either of my BFF's rave about you."

"Just because they don't rave, it doesn't mean they're not interested. You need to start paying closer attention to things, and only when you open your eyes will you really see what is going on with your friends."

"Right now I'm not interested in what is going on with my friends. I'm more interested in what is going on with my husband. I want to tell you some of the things I need from you too, and I hope that you don't take me the wrong way."

Cedric didn't respond. He sat back on the couch and faced me to listen.

"First, I've suspected for a long time that you've been having extramarital affairs. I don't have any proof that you have been, but if you are, I want you to end whatever it is that you have going on outside of our marriage. I also want you to think before you speak. Some of the things that you say to me are very harsh. I don't appreciate being disrespected by my own husband. You already know how I feel about your relationship with Jacoby, and I hope you're willing to do whatever to correct it. Lastly, I appreciate you for providing for us, but in addition to money, I need to be shown some love too. You rarely do anything spontaneous or kind for me anymore. I would be very appreciative if we could have sex more often. Is that asking for too much?"

Cedric pulled off his jacket and laid it on the arm of the couch. He looked at me with much seriousness in his eyes. "I'm going to say this to you one time and one time only. I am not cheating on you and I will never cheat on you. There are times when I flirt with women, talk to women or even have dinner with women. Sometimes, I do that shit to enhance my business relationships with them, but you have my word that I have not been intimate with any other woman than you.

"As for my mouth, what can I say other than it gets slick at times. You knew that before you married me, and depending on the situation, there are times when I can't control what I say. I will, however, try to control myself, but I can't make you any promises. I will work things out between me and Jacoby, but just remember what I said and back off. When it comes to us having sex, that's on you, baby. You've been the one holding back on the pussy, and I need to be presented with some spontaneous, thrilling shit too. You are just as boring as I am in the bedroom, so don't blame me for our sex life not being what it should be."

"I thought it wasn't what it should be because you've been intimate with other women. I want to believe you, Cedric, but it's so hard to when I know you have conversations with them, they call you, and you're always coming home late."

"Baby, I am late because I work hard to keep all of this you see around you. You need to stop assuming things and accusing me of doing stuff that I'm not doing. You have never caught me doing anything. It's so unfair to me if you're thinking all of that craziness in your head. That's where the problem lies between us. You need to get that craziness out yo' head and start giving me some credit."

Could I have been wrong about him? That was a possibility, especially since I had never caught him in the act doing anything. I had definitely been assuming a lot, only because my gut had been signaling that something was very wrong.

For now, I had to trust what Cedric had said. We agreed to work on our marriage and see what we could do better to repair it. The repair process started that night. While Cedric was in the shower, I hurried into my closet to put on something sexy. I opted for a ruby red, lace negligee with diamond studs that lined the breasts area. The negligee revealed most of my privates, including my nipples that were visible through the lace. The crotch section slipped between my shaved coochie lips, and the mountains on my smooth ass looked squeezable. I wanted to spice things up, so I lit some candles then dimmed the lights. I sprayed my body with dashes of sweet perfume, and then put on some slow, jazzy music to set the mood.

Cedric opened the doors to the bathroom with shock in his eyes. I smiled while lying sideways on the bed, where he had a clear view of my ass. He moistened his lips with his tongue then dropped the towel that was around his waist to the floor. His dick rose to its full potential and he glided up to the side of the bed.

"Now, that's what I'm talking about," he said, reaching out to rub my ass. He squeezed and massaged it, right along with my thick thighs. I had to turn my body around to face him, just so he could look between my legs and see what his touch was capable of doing to me. While he appeared to be in a trance, I switched positions on the bed and opened my legs. I felt the crotch of my negligee ease further into my slit and I suspected that Cedric got a glimpse of my moist folds.

"Sometimes," he said, "I forget how sexy you really are."

I felt the same way about him, but didn't say a word. Cedric rubbed his fingers against my walls then he pushed his fingers further inside, causing me to tighten my eyes and suck in a heap of air. I was on fire as he rotated his fingers inside of me, and my creamy fluids trickled between the crack of my ass. Seconds later, Cedric replaced his finger with his steel. It had been a while since we indulged ourselves, so I jerked slightly backward from the feel of his pleasing muscle.

"Don't act like you can't handle this," he said. "You've had it in your possession for years. You already know what to do with it."

Darn right I did. And once I got comfortable, I spread my legs wider, gripped his tight butt, and grinded my hips in circles. My glaze covered Cedric's entire shaft, and I toyed with my own clit while he watched. His eyes were filled with lust, and his deep strokes slowed as he attempted to calm his heartbeat and catch his breath.

"I—I don't know what to say about you, Kay. Other than you doing it, baby, you straight-up got that pussy doing the damn thing."

He didn't have to tell me, because I already knew it. I purposely stepped up my game. I wanted to let Cedric know that there was no reason for him to seek sexual pleasure elsewhere, especially when I was capable of providing him with all of the loving he needed. But I wasn't the only one at the top of my game. So was he. He had lifted me up from the bed and held me in his arms. My legs were secured around Cedric's waist as he backed me up to the wall and slammed his dick into me. I was going crazy as our naked bodies slapped together. My backside was being banged against the wall and when a picture fell, we both ignored it. I focused on the way he sucked my breasts and squeezed them. The way he grinded inside of me, milking my pussy for all that it could give to him. I wanted to give him more, but the dick was so good that my body weakened in his arms. My legs trembled and my fists pounded into the wall as I neared another orgasm.

"Give it to me, baby," Cedric said while lifting me to his broad shoulders. I held on tight and sprayed his lips with juices. He cleaned me up, but we were back at it again.

This time, I was bent over a chair, trying to catch my breath. We were still going at it when Jacoby came home. He knocked on the bedroom door to let us know he had made it in. I hoped that he didn't hear me screaming at the top of my lungs for Cedric to "fuck me harder," but I couldn't control the excitement my husband brought to the bedroom. This was long overdue. We had exhausted ourselves and Cedric wound up falling asleep with his dick resting comfortably inside of me.

The next day, I drove to Trina's apartment to see her. She seemed kind of quiet during dinner on Sunday, and she was known for always being the one who kept the conversation flowing. She also whispered to me that she needed to borrow some money, but I forgot to follow up with her. My mind was on other things that night, and they were also on what Cedric had said about her. He couldn't have been more wrong. If Trina was gay, I was born a dog.

I arrived at her apartment around noon. Trina did most of her art projects from her extra bedroom that she had turned into a studio. Her apartment was rather small, but she had given the place new life with colorful pictures and furniture. I knocked on the door. A few minutes later she opened it. She looked surprised to see me and she had a paintbrush in her hand. Her sweatpants had paint blotches on them and the tank shirt she wore revealed her toned arms. A scarf was wrapped around her hair, keeping it intact.

"What's been up with you and Evelyn's pop-up visits? First her, now you."

She widened the door to let me in. I could tell her comment was playful because she and Evelyn always showed up at my house unannounced too.

"I see you're busy painting and everything, but I stopped by because I wanted to find out what was going on with you. You also mentioned that you needed some money. How much?"

Trina closed the door and invited me into her living room to sit. "I'm doing okay. I just wish I didn't have to bother you about money all the time, but you know I don't have anywhere else to turn."

"I know and trust me when I say it's no bother. If the shoe were on the other foot, I know you'd do the same thing for me. Now, how much do you need?"

"Just a couple hundred dollars."

I removed my checkbook from my purse and wrote Trina a check for three hundred dollars. She smiled when I handed it over to her.

"Thank you. Now is there anything that I can do for you? You never ask me or Evelyn for anything. I want you to know that we're here for you as well."

"I get that, and all I need sometimes is somebody to talk to. I had some concerns with Cedric, but the two of us worked it out last night. I'm feeling much better now. I have a feeling that my marriage is back on track."

"That's good to know. After all that appeared to be going on with him and Jacoby, I thought Cedric found out about your little secret. He still doesn't know, does he?"

Hearing Trina speak of my secret caused my heart to drop to my stomach. This was something we weren't supposed to talk about. It was one of those things that needed to stay in the past.

"No, he doesn't know and he will never know that Jacoby isn't his son. They've had some issues lately that I expect them to work out real soon."

"I hope they do. You know, I always said your decision not to tell them the truth would come back and bite you in the butt one day. I hope I'm wrong."

Thinking about it was starting to give me a headache. I hurried to change the subject, and thought about what Cedric said to me about Trina last night.

"I know you're wrong, but anyway, can I tell you what Cedric had the audacity to say to me last night? It nearly floored me and I couldn't stop laughing."

"What? What did he say?"

"He said that he thought you were gay. His reason was because you never pay him any attention, and he said that you never show a connection with the men you bring around us. Now, tell me how full of himself my husband really is."

Trina shook her head and laughed. "Very much so full of himself. I don't see how you put up with his arrogant self, and for him to think such a thing is crazy. I am strictly dickly. There isn't anything that a woman can do for me. Period."

We high-fived each other and laughed again.

"I do think your husband is extremely fine, but I'm not the kind of person who will fall all out over a nice-looking man. I think that Cedric's ugly ways are what makes me not compliment his fineness, yet he may be onto something when he mentioned my connection with men. I tend to choose the wrong men. JaQuan and I had a disagreement before we got to your house, so we weren't speaking to each other that much. I'm not sure if I'm going to keep seeing him, and when I go into the studio tomorrow, I may call it off with him. I don't like how aggressive he is. When we have sex, he doesn't put enough into pleasing me."

"Yes, that's something that is very important, so I do know where you're coming from. I'm delighted that my arrogant and full-of-himself husband knows what he's doing in the bedroom. That's definitely a plus. Pertaining to the gay thing, I hope I didn't offend you. But in my opinion, I think two women sexing each other is so nasty. How can a woman give another sexual pleasure? I try not to judge people who get down like that, and I felt insulted when he spoke about you in that manner."

"I'm not offended at all. I think gays are pretty darn disgusting too. But what other people do in the privacy of their own homes is not any of my business. If they like it, I love it."

"Well, I don't like it or love it. But you're right. It has nothing to do with me."

Trina called me crazy and we continued to share good conversation. What I'd said didn't appear to bother her, but my friends were known for going back on things and calling you out on it later. I wasn't sure if Trina would throw this back at me later, but I was positive that somewhere down the road she would tell me that I hurt her feelings.

I left Trina's house around three o'clock. I wanted to get home to cook for Jacoby and Cedric, but when I got in the car I sat for a while, thinking. When Cedric and I were in college, I wanted to be with him so badly that I stopped taking my pills and did my best to get pregnant. But while I was seeing him, I had also been seeing someone else. His name was Arnez, but I didn't have feelings for him like I had for Cedric. Cedric had a good head on his shoulders, and I suspected that he would do right by his child and take good care of him. Arnez was a thug. He dropped out of college, had several other baby mamas and he started doing drugs. I knew Jacoby was his son, but I told Cedric the child was his. I stuck to my lie and the only people who knew the truth were Trina, Evelyn, and Arnez. They promised me that they would take my secret to their graves with them. I prayed that they would.

Chapter Six

Trina

As soon as the G-word left Kayla's mouth, my stomach tightened and my palms started to sweat. I did my best not to have a reaction that would alarm her, and the only thing that I could do was laugh. After she left, though, I cried. Cried because I didn't want to lie to her, but I had to. Why? Because, Kayla said it herself—being with another woman was nasty and she didn't understand how a woman could find sexual pleasure with another. She didn't get how we could love one another, so therefore, it would be a cold day in hell before I ever told anyone the truth.

Since I knew Cedric was suspicious, I had to do something to change his mind. That opportunity presented itself a few days later as I was sitting at a restaurant in the Central West End with the pastor's wife, Cynthia. Cedric walked in, but I hurried to shift my head in another direction.

"Who is that?" Cynthia asked. "You act as if you know him and don't want to be seen."

I had slumped down in my chair, but I wasn't sure if it had done me any good. Cedric kept looking around, but then he walked over to a table to join another woman. She wasn't all that great-looking and she definitely didn't have anything on my friend. I guess it could have been a business lunch, but there was too much smiling going on between them.

"Are you going to pay attention to what I said or are you going to focus on him?" Cynthia asked with snap in her voice.

"I heard everything you said, Cynthia. Just so you know, that's my friend's husband. I'm making sure everything is good, okay?"

"Oh, I see."

Cynthia turned in her seat to get a glimpse of the seemingly happy couple. I wanted to get the hell out of there, but if Cedric was going to be all up in my business, I had no problem getting in his.

"You said that you wanted to end things between us," I said to Cynthia. "Now you're singing a new tune. All I question is why?"

"Because I've been missing you, that's why. I'm having a difficult time moving on and I'm sure you can understand that, can't you?"

"I guess, but as long as you accept that I'm still involved with other people. You seemed a little irritated about me telling you that. I don't know why, especially since you're presenting yourself at church as being happily married."

"It's all for show, Trina. I seriously hate that man. I wish he would roll over and die so I can collect the money from his insurance policy. If you only knew the horrible things my husband has done. Then for him to stand there every Sunday morning and act like everything is all good is ridiculous."

Cynthia had some nerve. She was fake as all get-out and for a first lady, she had the sharpest tongue I had ever witnessed. Her bluntness was a real turnoff for me, but since I was only interested in sexual pleasure, I dealt with the crap.

"Pastor Clemons isn't the only one pretending. You should take a look in the mirror. The bottom line is we all have our issues. None of us are perfect. Not even him."

"I get that, so don't you start defending his actions. I hate speaking to you about him because you always act as if I'm the one in the wrong, not him. I say fuck him, and if you continue to take his side, fuck you too."

"Whatever, Cynthia. This isn't about who is right or who is wrong. You need to realize your own mistakes and stop blaming him so much for all that is going on between the two of you."

"I'm not blaming—"

Cynthia paused and looked behind me. When I turned my head, I saw Keith from work heading our way. He stood tall, was dark as midnight and handsome as ever. As always, his hair was cut into a sharply lined fade, and the artistic, colored tats on his muscular arms were what got my attention more than anything. I appreciated a creative man. I also admired one who sported a sexy goatee. With baggy jeans on, a leather belt holding them up, and a tank top that stretched across his ripped chest, I was so done with Cynthia. This conversation wasn't getting us anywhere.

Keith came up to the table. He was right on time. I introduced the two of them and invited Keith to join us, even though he said he was there waiting for his brother to show up. Cynthia was pissed. She stood up and snatched her purse off the table.

"When you have time, we'll talk further about what's going on. Enjoy the rest of your evening." She looked at Keith and shook his hand. "Nice meeting you, Keith. And, only if I wasn't married." Cynthia winked at him, laughed, and then walked away.

Keith blushed, but didn't say a word. I hated jealous women, and between Cynthia and Lexi I had my hands full. I enjoyed being with them, but they were both immature women who wanted to have our relationship their way or no way at all.

"So, why haven't you been to work?" Keith asked, turning the chair around, straddling it. "I haven't seen you around in several days."

I had been trying to avoid JaQuan. Thankfully, he had given up on calling me. "I've been working from home. Been getting a lot done and I'm preparing for the art show at the end of the month."

"Yeah, I am too. Been working my ass off. I'm looking forward to selling a lot of paintings that weekend. I need to get rid of some of the work I have stuck up in my house and there is plenty of it."

"I feel you. I'm anxious to get rid of some of my paintings too."

Keith's cell phone rang. He said it was his brother calling, so he answered. I looked over his shoulder at Cedric who was now clinking wineglasses with the lady. They were very talkative, but I was sure to get his attention, especially since Keith was now sitting with me.

"It's okay," Keith said. "If you're going to be that late, don't worry about it. Right now, I'm sitting across the table from a beautiful woman whose company I'm enjoying."

I smiled and he paused to listen to his brother. After Keith ended the call, he told me his brother wasn't going to make it.

"That's too bad," I said then laughed. I laughed loud enough for Cedric to turn his head, but he didn't.

"No, actually it's pretty good. After we get a quick bite to eat, maybe you'll invite me to your place so I can check out some of your paintings. Or I can always take you to my crib for you to check out mine."

I was so excited to see Cedric look away and lift his finger to get the waiter's attention. That was when I giggled and told Keith I would love for him to come to my place. Seduction was visible in my eyes, and from afar, I could finally see Cedric looking.

"Then let's hurry up and get this meal started," Keith teased. "How hungry are you?"

"Real hungry. So hungry that I think we should skip our meal and head out right now to my place."

Keith was all for it. He helped me finish the wine that Cynthia and I had been drinking and then we stood to go. I pretended to be tipsy. I giggled loudly again, and when I looked in Cedric's direction his eyes were glued to me. I smiled at him and held Keith's hand as I made my way over to the table where Cedric sat. He appeared uptight by my presence. I guess he figured I would call Kayla to tell her where he was. But friend or not, I didn't get down like that. I did my best to stay out of other people's business, and it had to be something real serious in order for me to get involved.

"I thought that was you over here, Cedric," I said, nearly rubbing my body against Keith's. "How are you?"

"I'm good. And you?"

"Fine. But . . . uh . . . this is Keith. Keith, this is my best friend's husband, Cedric."

They shook hands, but Cedric didn't dare introduce me to the woman sitting across the table from him with shock in her eyes. I didn't know if the *best friend's husband* announcement caught her off guard, or if jealousy had her eyes locked in that position.

"Enjoy the rest of your evening," Cedric said, trying to rush us off.

I looked up at Keith, who towered over me. I winked and turned my attention to Cedric again. "You bet we will. You have a wonderful evening too. Tell my girl I said hello, and I'm looking forward to dinner again. This time, you all can come to my place. Maybe I'll talk Keith into cooking something real delightful for everyone."

Cedric nodded. "Maybe so. Be sure to talk to *her* about it and let me know."

I started to check his ass for referring to his wife as *her*, but I left well enough alone. I had shown him that it was possible for me to make a connection with a man, and I was so sure that Cedric's eyes were still on us as we left the restaurant, appearing real cozy. My only problem was: How I was going to get out of this? Yes, Keith was fine-slash-sexy as fuck, but I didn't want to have sex with him. He was looking forward to something. I could tell by the glare in his eyes.

We stood next to my car with no breathing room in between us. "I guess I'm following you, right?" he said.

"I guess you are. Go get your car and I'll be right here waiting for you."

"My car is parked in the parking garage around the corner. I may be a minute, but I'm coming."

"Sure. I'll be waiting right here in my car. Hurry."

Keith walked away, and as soon as he was out of my sight, I hurried into my car and sped off. Almost ten minutes later, he was ringing my cell phone. I didn't answer, but the next time I saw him I was sure I had some explaining to do.

Within thirty minutes I was home. Unfortunately for me, though, Cynthia was parked outside in her car waiting for me and Lexi was waiting in her car. I was not in the mood to explain myself to anyone, and I certainly didn't want them going at it with each other. Their personalities would clash, so I just kept it moving, hoping that they didn't see me.

My only other options were to either go to Evelyn's place or Kayla's. By the time I sat around with them talking and wasting time, I was sure Lexi and Cynthia would be gone. Then again, maybe not, especially since Lexi was more persistent than Cynthia was.

I made up my mind and drove to Evelyn's place. I squeezed my car in between two vans, but as I got ready to exit the car my cell phone rang. It was Keith calling again. I felt terrible for dissing him like I did, so I answered as if I were in a rush.

"Please, please forgive me," I said in a fake panic. "As soon as you left, my sister called and said my father had been rushed to the hospital because of a heart attack. I'm here now, trying to see what's going on. Can I call you back later?"

"Su—sure, Trina. Take care and if you need anything let me know."

"I will. Thanks."

I shut my phone off and sighed from relief. I wasn't sure if he believed me or not, but it was the best I could do for right now. As for my father, he was a deadbeat any damn way. I hadn't seen him in years, so I didn't feel bad about the lie I had told.

I opened the car door to get out. But the moment my heel touched the pavement, I spotted a familiar car coming in my direction. There weren't too many people driving around in a steel-gray Mercedes with tinted windows and a personalized license plate. At first, I assumed that Kayla was behind the wheel. But, when Cedric got out, my brows shot up. Shock washed across my face as I watched him smooth walk his way to the elevator and swipe a card to get in. I wasn't sure if he was heading to Evelyn's loft or not. Security was tight in her building and she had to personally let her guests in.

Cedric, however, had his own access. I was curious about what was going on, so I waited for fifteen minutes until I got out of my car and went to the elevator. I punched in Evelyn's code. A few seconds later she appeared on the screen.

"What's up, *chicka*?" I said. "I just stopped by to see what you were up to. Do you feel like company?"

Evelyn raked her fingers through her hair. Her eyes were shifty. I could tell something was up, and it didn't take long for me to realize that Cedric was there with her. *Why?* was the real question.

"You know what," she said, then released a fake cough. "I'm not feeling well right now, Trina. Can I call you tomorrow? I really want to get some rest."

"No problem. I'll call you tomorrow—or better yet, I look forward to seeing you at lunch. Until then, I hope you feel better."

Evelyn displayed a fake smile then she disappeared from the screen. I got in my car and left. All kinds of thoughts were swarming in my head. Was I wrong for thinking that Cedric and Evelyn were fucking? I mean, why else would he be here at eight o'clock in the evening? And whatever happened to his date? Maybe she got upset with him or maybe she wasn't his date after all. I was left with plenty of questions, but maybe they were questions that I didn't want answers to. Kayla surely had her hands full. It was in my best interest to keep quiet and not hit her with accusations. If she said she and Cedric were getting back on the right track, I had to accept that and let them work on their marriage.

Chapter Seven

Evelyn

I was in bed watching TV when I heard the door squeak open. I heard his shoes hit the floor, and when Cedric stood in the doorway to my bedroom, I wasn't surprised or excited about seeing him. The last deposit into my account had me shaken up. I had been leaving him plenty of messages, but he hadn't returned my phone call. To say I was upset would've been an understatement. He could tell by the blank expression on my face that I wanted him out.

But as soon as I opened my mouth to speak, that was when someone buzzed me from outside. It was Trina. I had to hurry to the door and get rid of her. I was pleased that she didn't question me and I was glad that she didn't push to come in.

After turning her away, I moved away from the screen and rolled my eyes as I walked past Cedric in my white silk robe. He grabbed my wrist and swung me around.

"What in the hell is wrong with you?" he asked. "Why all the attitude?"

"You know what's wrong with me," I hissed. "If you don't, check your cell phone and see. Better yet, check my account and you'll really see."

I snatched my wrist away from him and rushed into the bedroom. Cedric came after me and pushed me on the bed. I fell on my stomach, right on the edge of the bed.

He lay on top of me, pressing his body against mine so I couldn't move.

"I've been busy. I didn't have time to answer all thirty-nine of your bullshit messages. How dare you get upset with me about money? If I could calculate all that I've given you, you know damn well that you have no reason to be talking shit. You make me feel as though all I'm good for is feeding your damn bank account. Can't we get together one fucking time without you asking me for money? Just one time, Evelyn, and you don't always have to ask to receive."

"Shut the fuck up talking to me and get out of here. You're not the only one who gives a lot and—"

"No, you shut the fuck up! All you give me is pussy and a goddamn headache, every time I leave here. I don't know why I keep coming here and fucking with you like this. I'm much better off at home with Kayla. At least she don't gripe as much as yo' ass do."

I tried to turn around and slap the shit out of him for comparing me to Kayla. The comparisons hurt, but as I tried to express my anger, he continued to hold me down. He lifted himself just a little and pulled my robe up to expose my ass. He then lowered himself and slithered the tip of his curled tongue down the crack of my butt. His touch tickled and felt good at the same time. My resistance stopped when he separated my butt cheeks and started to taste me while down on his knees. My breathing slowly increased and my eyes fluttered then shut.

"I—I'm so sorry for stressing you," I whined between deep breaths. "I get—get lonely at times and I need you here with me. I want more, Cedric, *waaaay* more of you—this, all of it. I'm so jealous that Kayla has you, and all that you give to her and—and I wish this could be about us and she—she was no longer in the picture. You're *soooo* good to me, and my *puuuussy* gushes over the way you make it feel. I l*oooove* how you do that shit, and I'm ... I'm *cuuuumming!*"

Cedric held my hips and licked faster as I covered his lips with my sweet icing. It took a few minutes for me to regroup then I rushed off the bed to rip off his clothes. I dropped to my knees and sucked his dick into my mouth. It soothed the back of my throat, and it wasn't long before he sprayed my mouth with his fluids. I swallowed his energy drink then fell back on the bed. Cedric stood at the end of it and spread my legs wide. He beat his dick on my pussy to get hard again. It grew to great heights, and as he slipped it into me, he rocked our bodies at a fast pace that caused my firm breasts to wobble around. I couldn't get enough of this man. My need for his overly satisfying dick was starting to supersede my need for his money.

Cedric spread my legs even wider and he grinded so hard that I was on the brink of cumming again. "You like this shit, don't you, bitch!" he shouted. "I appreciate all that bullshit you be talking, but don't be jealous. This dick ain't going nowhere but in this juicy pussy, inside of that pretty ass of yours and back in your mouth. Until then, throw that pussy to me so I can catch it."

I threw it and Cedric caught it. We indulged ourselves that night, and by morning I could barely walk straight. I was scheduled to meet Kayla and Trina for lunch, and when I limped into the restaurant, feeling as if Cedric's dick was still inside of me, they both stared at me.

"What's wrong with you?" Kayla asked, wincing. "Are you all right?"

I plopped down in the chair and crossed my legs to calm the soreness. "Nothing is wrong with me. I'm just tired and my boss has been working me like crazy today."

"Are you still sick?" Trina asked. "You looked terrible last night. I was worried about you."

"I'm feeling a little better. I was so out of it last night. I meant to call you, but I knew I'd see you today." I picked up the menu, looking at it. "Have y'all ordered yet? I only have five bucks on me, so I may have to order some soup or something."

"No problem," Kayla rushed to say. "You know I got you. Order whatever you want to."

In that case, when the waiter came over to take our orders I ordered a cheeseburger and some fries. I hadn't splurged like that since our dinner engagement, and I didn't even have money to buy groceries. While we were sitting at the table, I used my phone to check my bank account status. Maybe Cedric would surprise me and throw some money in my account. But when I checked, all I saw was red. My account was at a negative thirty dollars. Payday was tomorrow, so I released a deep sigh, trying not to trip.

"Okay," Kayla said, rubbing her hands together. "I need y'all help with something."

She reached into her purse and pulled out several vacation brochures. "I want to surprise Ceddy with a vacation. The other day we talked about sprucing up our marriage and I think we should start with a relaxing vacation. Tell me which one of these resorts looks and sounds the most interesting. It's been a while since we've been on a vacation together and he really needs one."

Was she seriously over there bragging about a vacation when my ass was broke? She knew Trina didn't have any money, either, and how dare Kayla be so selfish and make this lunch meeting all about her? Trina picked up the brochures to look at them, but I didn't even bother. I pretended to be occupied with something on my phone, and then I sent *Ceddy* a text message, telling him how spectacular last night was.

"You can never go wrong with Hawaii," Trina said. "But these vacation packages for Sandals look very interesting too. What do you think, Evelyn?"

"I think . . ." I paused when my phone alarmed me that I had a message. When I looked at it, Cedric had sent me a picture of his hard dick. I snickered and read his comment: Still hard, thinking about last night. Can't wait 2 see you again!

My pussy thumped from the thought. I smiled then continued with the conversation. "As I was saying, I think Cedric wouldn't have a good time. Instead of spending his money, why don't you just plan something simple? Most men like to keep it simple. The vacation thing is more about you, Kayla, than it is about him."

Her face scrunched from my comment. "No, it's not. And it'll do us good to get away. All I asked was for you to help me choose. I don't think you know Cedric enough to comment on what he would or wouldn't like. All you know about him is what I tell you."

Was this bitch a fool or a damn fool? I knew Cedric better than she did. If she believed that he was trying to work on their marriage, I felt sorry for her. I didn't get how a woman could spend years and years with a man, yet be so blind and not see what was going on around her. Kayla was setting herself up for a huge downfall. One day I was going to have a little pleasure of watching her come down from the high horse she had been on.

I only had an hour for lunch, but after spending thirty to forty minutes talking about what Ceddy had been up to, I was ready to go. I gobbled down my burger and finished every last fry. I was so full from eating so much that my stomach felt tight. I air-kissed Trina and Kayla's cheeks before telling them I had to get back to work.

"You look like you need to go back home and get some rest," Trina said. "Don't you have some vacation time left from work?"

"I do, but my vacation isn't scheduled until later this year. I said I'll be fine, and I only have a few more hours left anyway."

"Well, go ahead and get out of here," Kayla said. "If you want me to, I'll stop by later to bring you some soup and flu medicine. I know you say you're fine, but you don't look well to us."

"Whatever, Kayla, do what you wish. I gotta go. I'll see the two of you soon."

I walked off, but as soon as I made it back to the office a sheen of sweat covered my forehead. My stomach felt queasy. I rushed to the bathroom and could feel vomit creeping up my throat. The toilet was piled high with my lunch and with the orange juice I drank earlier. I wiped my mouth with a napkin then splashed water on my face to cool off. I left the bathroom to tell my boss that I needed to go home, but he asked me to come into his office and close the door.

"Have a seat, Evelyn, this won't be long."

I took a seat and stared at Mr. Payne from across his desk. He was a grumpy old white man with a toupee sitting crookedly on his head. His gray eyes were frightening, and the buttons on his shirt were about to pop off due to his potbelly that could be seen a mile away.

"You can go home, but unfortunately, you may have to stay there. Today will be your last day. We can't keep employing people who we consider troublemakers. We've gotten too many complaints about you, Evelyn. Too many and I've ignored those complaints for long enough."

I sat in shock with my eyes bugged and my jaw dropped. Tears welled in my eyes, but I blinked to clear them. "Complaints? What complaints are you talking about?"

"Letters that show you've been harassing some of your coworkers. One coworker said you keyed her car and scripted your initials, another one said you flattened her tires and wrote her a nasty letter. I don't know what you have against the white women who work here, but this obviously isn't the place for you."

I seriously could have fallen out of my chair. I had no idea what he was talking about and this whole damn thing sounded like a setup. "Mr. Payne, if you received that many complaints about me, why didn't you say anything to me? You never questioned me or gave me a warning. I have no clue what you're talking about and I have never done anything to anyone in here. I'd like to see the letters you're talking about. I would also like to talk to the people who complained about me. Something isn't adding up here. I have nothing against white women, period."

Mr. Payne reached inside of his desk drawer and pulled out two letters. He gave them to me. All I could do was shake my head. The letters referred to the women as white sluts who I hated with a passion. According to the letter, I threatened them and promised to do more damage if they told on me. The letters had my signature and it was so identical to mine that it was scary.

"This . . . this is not from me." I wiped a slow tear that trickled down my face. "I swear it isn't me. Why would I write something like that and then sign my name to it?"

"I don't know, but either way, I need for you to go. We'll investigate this more, but for now you need to vacate the premises until this matter is resolved."

I surely wanted to tell Mr. Payne to kiss my ass, but I figured there was a possibility that I would have to come back and kiss his. It was times like this when I wished that I could afford a lawyer. EEOC was another option too. But for now, I packed up my belongings and left without causing a scene.

While in the car, I wondered who had written those letters. Who in the hell was out to get me and why? Had the white women conspired to do harm to me? They were all so jealous of me, and I saw the way many of them looked at me with jealousy in their eyes. But the other women were all haters too. I never befriended any of them. All I ever did was go to work and come home. My measly paychecks were nothing to brag about, and the headache all of this had caused wasn't worth it.

For now, I needed Cedric more than I had ever needed him before. I had to ask him for more money. He was the only one who could save me. I reached for my cell phone and punched in his number.

"I'm on my way to a meeting," he said. "Make it quick."

"Are you coming over tonight? I need to talk to you about something very important."

"Talk or play? I'm sure we won't be talking all night, will we?"

"No. We can play too, just come, okay?"

"See you around eight or nine, maybe sooner. It depends on whenever I can get out of here."

"Okay. I'll be waiting."

I drove home in a daze. I hoped that Cedric would be able to help me. This would be the first time I had to ask him for a staggering amount like fifty-thousand dollars to make up for the losses I was about to incur. Damn!

Chapter Eight

Jacoby

I tried not to poke my nose where it didn't belong and stay out of grown-folks' business, but sitting on the sidelines was something that I couldn't do. I was so upset with my mother for acting as if she didn't have any fucking sense at all and I hated my father with a passion. I saw right through his bullshit. I wondered why my mother hadn't opened her eyes and realized how much she was getting played. This was ridiculous. I was so upset the other night when I heard the two of them fucking. I mean, what good was that going to do? What was the purpose and what kind of marriage were they representing? I was so outdone and had felt this way for a very long time. Thing is, I was told to keep my mouth shut. My mother wasn't trying to hear it and neither was Cedric. That's why I was doing what I could do to change this situation around and it started with Evelyn.

A blind person could see that she was fucking around with my father. Anyone paying attention would know and it was as if neither of them cared who found out. I'd seen them at dinners, at her house, at his office, and even at my house. She had the audacity to come into our home to fuck my father, and when my mother went to Atlanta last year, that same night, Evelyn was there. They thought I was asleep, but I wasn't. I saw it all, as I had seen it every time I went somewhere with my father. I didn't understand his obsession with women. It was as if he could never get enough.

Me, I'd had enough. I did my best to get Evelyn fired. I wanted her to feel some of the hurt I'd been feeling. She was out to destroy my parents, but I wanted to destroy her. This was just a start, and I assumed that her little situation at work would be dealt with real soon. I also wanted to get my father where it hurt, but I had to be careful with him. He was a smart man. He could always sense when something wasn't right. For now, the least I could do was have a man-to-man conversation with him. Let him know how I was feeling about all of this shit and encourage him to knock it off before it was too late. If I couldn't get through to him today, I wasn't sure where I would turn.

I had a half day at school, so I drove by my father's office to see if he was there. As I was looking for a parking spot, I spotted him leaving his office. He met up with a woman I had seen him with plenty of times before. The two of them shared brief words and a quick kiss before she got into my father's car. Before getting inside, his eyes scanned the parking lot while he unbuttoned his suit jacket. He then hung it on a hook in the backseat and I saw him unbutton his cuffs so he could raise his sleeves. Afterward, he got in the car and sped off. I followed closely behind. I figured they were headed to their usual place, which was in a nearby parking garage where she often gave him a blow job. There were times when they'd had sex too. I had pictures to prove it, and hurtful or not, I would one day show my mother who the real liar was.

My father parked his car in a reserved spot that belonged to him. My car was parked several rows over, but I could see him pull out the newspaper, as if he were reading it. The woman next to him disappeared. To his lap she went and there appeared to be some maneuvering around going on. Once things got settled, I watched from afar. I tried to give the motherfucker time to bust his nut, but then I thought it would be best for me to interrupt him.

I cocked my hat on backwards and eased my hands in my jean pockets as I made my way up to his car. I figured he saw me in his rearview mirror, because the newspaper lowered and the woman with him jumped up from his lap. As I bent over, he lowered his window. I glared inside. My father appeared calm as ever, but the woman wiped her lips and kept looking at me with bugged eyes.

"Can I help you?" Cedric said.

"We need to talk?"

"Right now? Can't you see I'm busy?"

"You're always busy, but it's either now or never. I prefer now because I have some shit that I need to get off my chest."

Cedric unlocked the car. "Get inside. Make this quick, Jacoby. I need to get back to work."

Work my ass. I sat on the backseat, behind him. I swear if I had a rope or something close to it, I would have used that opportunity to choke his ass. I was starting to hate him that much.

My father looked over at the woman sitting next to him. "Just in case you don't know, that's my son. His timing is way off, but I would be pleased if you wouldn't mind finishing what you already started."

The woman spoke to me then wiped her lips again. "Are you sure?" she said. "You . . . you want me to continue with your son in the car?"

He looked at me in the rearview mirror. "Why not? It ain't like he ain't never had his dick sucked before. I'm sure that he loves pussy just as much as I do. Right, son?"

I wanted to throw up. Whether I liked that shit or not, he didn't even have to go there with this trick. Her stupid ass didn't hesitate to drop back into his lap, and I kept thinking to myself what a fool she was.

My father pressed the back of his head against the headrest and closed his eyes. "What's on your mind, Jacoby? Speak."

I didn't hesitate. "What's on my mind is I want you to stop this. Don't you know how much damage you're doing to our family? And what about Mother? Why are you doing this to her? I mean, I don't get it. If you don't want to be with her, why don't you just divorce her? That way, we can all get on with our lives and you can do whatever it is that you want to do."

He opened his eyes and shrugged his shoulders. "I'm doing what I want to do regardless. And to answer all of your questions, I'll shoot one word to you and hope that you understand. Timing. Timing is everything. I'll divorce your mother when I get ready to. As for right now, I'm not ready to make that move."

The slurping sounds of the woman sucking his dick were very distracting. She lifted her head to reply to his comment. "I hope you're ready soon. You told me that you—"

He grabbed the back of her head and pulled her hair tight. "Keep your fucking mouth shut and stay out of this conversation between me and my son. You can do so by focusing more on making me bust this nut, and just so you know, I'm nowhere near that yet. Ya feel me?"

She nodded and resumed sucking his dick. "That's my girl," he said while patting the back of her head. "*Deeeeep.* Go deep."

I released a deep sigh and shook my head. We caught each other's eyes in the rearview mirror and I could see the smirk on his face. He was definitely getting a kick out of this.

"Don't look so disappointed, son. See, when you accrue all of the money that I have over the years, you'll be able to do this kind of shit too. It's called having power over the pussy. Women will flock to you and you'll be able to get them to do whatever in the fuck you want them to do. They will love your dirty drawers and all they'll want from time to time is a little cash and a hard, satisfying dick. That's all your mother ever wanted from me, so don't be upset with me if she got exactly what she asked for." He paused and shut his eyes. "Umph. You on to something, baby. I likes that shit—damn it, girl, slow down!"

He started lifting himself from the seat, pumping the woman's mouth that was full with his goods. He seemed so into it that I doubted he was paying me any attention. My fists were tightened. I swear that I wanted to knock him upside his head, just because. I wanted to scream and release all of this anger inside of me, but I figured that would do me no good. My father would never see things my way. He would never understand the damage behind his actions. I felt as if I had wasted my time, so I was ready to let him get back to "work."

I shook the headrest to make him open his eyes. When he stared at the rearview mirror, I looked at him and spoke. "Ju—just think about what I'm saying to you. Enough is enough, and I'm losing so much respect for you. There was a time when you were real good to me, man, but you've been on my back and coming down on me, knowing damn well why I'm so angry with you. I can't control my anger. All of this is upsetting to me, and I . . . I want my parents to love, honor, and respect each other. That's all I want. If y'all can't do that then walk away from each other. I don't care who you're with, not even with Evelyn. My mother deserves better than this. Deep down, I think you know that."

He bit into his lip and squeezed his hands on the steering wheel. When the woman lifted her head, I turned mine to look out the window. I figured her mouth was filled with his semen, and I surely didn't want to see it.

"*Ahhhhh*," he said then sighed. "I—I've always been good to you, son, but unfortunately, there are a few things that you don't understand right now. One day you will. When that day comes, you and I will be on the right path. I figured that you knew about me and Evelyn, but like all the rest, she don't mean shit to me. If anybody deserves better, it's me. I deserve better, and deep down, that's the only truth that I know."

I opened the car door and placed one foot on the ground. I then turned to the woman who appeared hurt by Cedric's words, but kept her mouth shut.

"I guess we all need to wake up and know our self-worth," I said, directing my comment to her. I then looked at the back of Cedric's head. "Money or not, you shouldn't treat people the way you do. And whatever it is that I need to understand, I wish someone would lay it on the line and tell me. As of right now, I don't get it. You're the worst fucking father on this earth and I wish that when your whole world come tumbling down, that I'll have a front-row seat."

"Well, for now, yo' ass is in the back. Thanks for the father-son talk, but I need to head back to the office. See you at home, son, and I wish you had more time. Time for my princess over here to give you some of that action that she just gave me. Maybe it'll help to knock off that chip on your shoulder, and trust me when I say that every man needs a little relaxation from time to time."

I didn't have anything else to say. I slammed the car door, feeling as if I could kill him.

Chapter Nine

Kayla

After Evelyn left the restaurant, Trina and I stayed for at least another thirty minutes or so. She was telling me about her experience with Keith and said that she was starting to feel something for him.

"I don't know what it is," she said. "He's different. When he came over last night, we made love. I was in another world with him, and I appreciated how he took his time with me. I think he could be the one."

"I'm glad to hear that, and I'll be so glad when either you or Evelyn get married. Sometimes, I feel so out of place in this friendship. I'm always talking about me and my husband, feeling as if the two of you can't relate. Aside from that, it'll be good for you to settle down. I'm pleased that you haven't given up on love."

Trina smiled and ate a piece of the pecan pie she'd ordered. "So, what's your take on Evelyn?" she asked. "She was so out of it today, wasn't she?"

"Yes, she was. I could tell something was wrong with her, but I guess she didn't want to say what it was. I'm going to stop by her place later to check on her. I'll probably take her some soup and orange juice, just in case she needs it."

"From the way she was looking she definitely needs it. I'm starting to worry about her a lot. I'm worried about you as well. I don't mean to pry, but are you sure your marriage with Cedric is on the right track? There is something about him that I—"

"I know. Something about him that you don't like. I get that, Trina, but Cedric is an awesome man and decent husband. He's not perfect, but he's trying to do better. I don't say a lot to you and Evelyn about our situation because I don't want y'all judging me. I don't want you to despise him, either, and please know that I'm a big girl who is capable of dealing with the man I married. So, don't worry about me. I already told you that things are starting to get better. He sent me a dozen beautiful roses earlier, and I have a feeling that tonight is going to be real special for us."

Trina had a peculiar look on her face that I couldn't read. I wasn't sure why she was so worried about me, and I figured her opinion about Cedric had changed, especially after him saying that he believed she was gay. Maybe I shouldn't have said anything to her.

As I was in thought, she reached over and placed her hand on top of mine. "As your friend, all I'm saying to you is: Know who to trust and who not to. Keep your eyes and ears open and pay attention to your surroundings. Listen to your gut and don't allow love for anyone to destroy you."

"I appreciate the advice and the same goes for you."

Trina finished her pie. Shortly thereafter, we went our separate ways. I stopped by the grocery store to pick up a few things for Evelyn. Then I went home to check on Jacoby. He was there doing his homework while watching TV.

"I'm on my way to Evelyn's place," I said, standing next to him in the kitchen. "Do you want anything to eat before I go?"

He shrugged with such a disappointed look on his face. "I'll just throw a TV dinner in the microwave. And if you don't mind, I'd like to take Adrianne to the movies tonight."

"I don't mind, but you know it's a school night. Don't stay out too late and be sure to take your time on your homework."

"I will. And—uh—by the way, tell Evelyn I said hello."

"I sure will. But I want you to perk up. Things aren't that bad, are they?"

Jacoby stared at me for a few minutes and then he placed his hands behind his head. "Since we're living in this fantasy world, I guess things aren't bad at all. But what do you think?"

"I think I need to go see about my friend. Don't forget what I said, and no matter how bad you may think things are, I will always love you."

I started to walk away, but I turned around when I thought about Cedric. "Did your father speak to you about going on a business trip with him yet?"

"No. I don't want to go on a dumb business trip with him, and he can forget about asking me that crap."

I went back over to the table and touched Jacoby's back. "Don't be like that, Jacoby. Give your father a chance to make things right. He's trying. He really wants to make peace with you. He can't if you continue to have up a brick wall. So when he inquires about going places with him, at least think about it first."

"I don't have to think about anything because my answer will always be no. The peace that I get is when he's away from here. That's all the peace I need."

I released a deep breath and swallowed the lump that felt stuck in my throat. Jacoby was being difficult when he didn't have to be.

"You're going to ruin your relationship with your father, and one day you're going to regret it. For the sake of our family staying together and being happy, please

reconsider and think hard about how you can improve
your relationship with him. You are too stubborn, Jacoby.
It's time to let go of the bitterness you have inside and
move on."

Jacoby sucked his teeth and narrowed his eyes. "Move
on? Really? If I am bitter, it's because he made me this
way. I'm not as forgiving as you are, Mother, and I don't
enjoy being around my father as much as you do. All he
does is disrespect you when I go places with him. I don't
like how he looks at other women and—"

"Stop it right there, okay? A married man is allowed to
look at other women, as long as he doesn't touch. Hell,
I look at other men, but it doesn't mean that I love your
father any less. You're finding excuses as to why you don't
want to get your relationship with your father on the right
track. That's a shame, Jacoby. A darn shame and I'm real
disappointed in you."

I walked off, but halted my steps when Jacoby shouted
at me.

"Disappointed in me! Well, guess what? I'm disappointed in you too. The question is when are you going to
wake the fuck up? When are you going to see my father
for who he really is? I don't want to be around him,
especially not when I have to go to so-called 'business
meetings' with him and listen to him fucking other
women in the next room. He's been doing more than just
looking. I *have* lost all respect for him, and I'm about to
lose it for you too!"

I rushed up to Jacoby and slapped him across his face.
"Lower your voice and don't you ever speak to me that
way! To hell with the movies. When you get done with
your homework, go to your room and think about how
you're going to work on that bad attitude of yours."

Jacoby got out of his chair and hurried past me. He
went into his room, and not listening to a word I said, he

ran out of the house and got into his car. I went after him, but couldn't catch him. Mad as hell, I hurried back inside to call Cedric.

"Yes, Kay," he said with a sigh, as if he were busy.

"I'm sorry to bother you, but Jacoby just ran out of here, upset. I tried to stop him, but I don't know where he's gone."

"What is he upset for this time?"

"I asked if he would join you on the business trip you mentioned and he said that he didn't want to go because your trips turn personal and women are involved. He then started yelling and cursing at me, so I slapped him. I don't know what is happening. . . ." I paused to wipe my tears. I had never put my hands on my son, but his words to me were so hurtful.

"Calm down, all right? Jacoby needs some time to get his head straight. I assure you that he'll be back soon. I keep telling you that he's just at that age right now where he wants to be the boss and he doesn't want to listen. I used to act the same way as a teenager, especially when things didn't go how I wanted them to. As for my business trips, he's just bitter and he'll say anything to upset you. Stop letting him get to you like that. The moment I get home tonight, I'll have a talk with him. I promise you that things won't get out of hand, and I'll listen to whatever he has to say."

I swallowed again and nodded. "Okay. I'll see you when you get home. I'm glad we had a chance to talk. I feel better."

Cedric laughed, only to make me laugh. "Good. Now can I get back to work?"

"Please do."

After we ended our call, I wasn't going to go over to Evelyn's place, but since I had already bought her fruit, soup, and juices, I decided to go. It was a little after five o'clock. Since she got off work at four, I assumed she was at home. With a grocery bag in my hand, I punched in her code. Minutes later, she appeared on the screen, looking at me.

"Yes," she said.

"Buzz me in. I have something for you."

"Whatever it is, I don't want it. I don't feel up to company right now, so please go."

I could tell Evelyn had been crying from the puffiness in her eyes. "I'm not leaving, so you may as well buzz me in. I want to know why you're so upset, and stop shutting me out like this. Have you forgotten that I'm your best friend?"

Evelyn disappeared from the screen then she buzzed me in. The elevator opened and I took it up to her floor. When I got off, I could see that her door was cracked. I opened the door and saw her lying on the couch in skimpy boy shorts and a white wife-beater. Her nipples were poking through it and her hair was wildly scattered on her head. Beads of sweat dotted her body and her entire place felt like heat was delivered straight from hell. I put the bag on the counter and walked over to the thermostat.

"What in the heck is going on with you?" I asked then clicked the thermostat on cool.

"Don't bother," she said. "My electric was turned off today. The air doesn't work."

"How . . . why is your electric turned off? Didn't you pay your bill?"

Evelyn sat up on the couch and wiped snot from her nose with a tissue. "I didn't have enough to pay it. I called for an extension, but they wouldn't give it to me."

"That's ridiculous."

I walked over to the windows to open them. There wasn't much of a breeze stirring, but it was so stuffy inside that I needed some fresh air. I sat on the couch next to Evelyn, clenching her hand with mine.

"If you needed some money for your electric bill, all you had to do was ask me. Now go get your bill and let me call the electric company to make your payment. They will turn it right back on, won't they?"

"Probably not until tomorrow. This has to be the worst day of my life. To make a long story short, I also got fired today. My whole world is tumbling down. I don't know what I'm doing wrong or what I can do to stop all of this crap from happening to me."

I felt horrible for her. I didn't understand why she hadn't told me things were this bad. "Fired? Fired for what? And your world is not tumbling down. Most things can be fixed and you're just going through a difficult time."

"I was let go because of coworker complaints. Obviously, the women there don't like me and they conspired to get me fired."

I shook my head and silently thanked God for being in a position where I didn't have to involve myself with some of the crazy people in corporate America. "That's terrible. But you'll find another job, so don't worry. Just go get your electric bill and let's get this thing paid for."

Evelyn wiped her nose again and dabbed her watery eyes. She stood up and went to her bedroom. I couldn't help but notice how shapely she was. And she was slim. Her body didn't have an ounce of fat on it. I had way more curves than she did, and according to her I was thick.

While she was in the bedroom getting her bill, I went into the kitchen to put up the groceries. I opened the fridge and the only thing inside was a bottle of diet Coke. It was empty as ever. I felt terrible for not realizing how badly my best friend had been suffering. I wish I had gotten her some more groceries, and I made a mental note to come back tomorrow to bring her some more things. I put the fruit and juice in the refrigerator then put the cans of soup in the cabinets. They were pretty bare too, causing me to shake my head even more.

Evelyn came back into the living room and sat on the couch. I poured her a glass of orange juice, but when I looked in the trash can to throw the bag away, I noticed a pregnancy test inside. I blinked several times, looking at the positive sign that was clearly visible. A smile washed across my face as I carried the orange juice over to her.

"What are you smiling for?" she said in a soft tone. She took the glass from my hand and gave me her electric bill.

"I'm smiling because I see somebody is about to be a mommy." My voice screeched and I reached over to give Evelyn a hug. "Why didn't you tell me? Oh my God, I can't believe you're pregnant! How could you consider this the worst day of your life, after finding out you're pregnant?"

Evelyn didn't appear as excited as I was. She slowly nodded and gazed at the trash can in the kitchen. "I—I just took the test today. I wanted to wait until the doctor confirmed it, before I said anything."

"Those tests are pretty accurate. I—I don't know what else to say, other than I'm so happy for you."

Evelyn shrugged and sort of rolled her eyes. "I'm sorry if I'm not as excited about this as you are, but this is a bad time for me. A child is not what I want to bring into this mess I have going on right now."

I reached for her hands again, holding them with mine. "Listen, I know you're going through a lot, but this will all work itself out. That child is a blessing to you and don't you ever forget that. I'll help you get back on your feet, but you have to promise me that you'll get back to work and get out of this slump you're in. I hate seeing you like this. It pains me that you didn't share with me what has been going on with you. Why didn't you tell me you needed help?"

Evelyn removed her hands from mine and plopped back on the couch. She massaged her forehead and closed her eyes. "Because, I get tired of coming to you for every single thing. You already have a full plate and I knew Trina had just hit you up for some cash. I suspect that Cedric doesn't know about all this money exchanging hands, and isn't he going to be upset with you for giving us his money?"

"At the end of the day, his money is my money too. He never questions what I do with it because he knows that I'm responsible. It's not like I'm out here blowing a lot of money. I'm very careful about how much I spend. You know how I used to run to the malls every day and do all that crazy stuff that rich women do? I don't go out like that anymore, because material things don't bring about the happiness my heart desires. Seeing my best friends on their feet and doing well makes me feel good. Knowing that my son's college is paid for delights me, and having a husband who I can trust is what's important. Now tell me, my dear, longtime, beautiful friend, how far in debt are you?"

Evelyn bit into her nails and widened her eyes as she looked at me. "I'm too embarrassed to say."

"Tell me. Now!"

"Almost two-hundred thousand dollars in debt, but that includes student loan money that I have yet to start paying on. Minus that and the interest money, about a hundred thousand in debt."

I put my hand on my hip. "With no mortgage, you should know better. But here's what I'm going to do."

I told Evelyn that I would give her twenty-five-thousand dollars for the next four months to help her. She agreed to call the student loan provider to make arrangements on her bill. She also agreed to find another job, and I offered to help with lawyer fees because the situation on her job sounded fishy. By the time I got ready to leave, she was all smiles. She appeared better and she seemed more upbeat about the baby.

"So what does Marc have to say?" I asked. "He is the father, isn't he?"

"He—he seems excited. I just told him today and he said that he hoped it would be a boy. I'm hoping for one too."

"Either one will suit me just fine. I can't believe I'm going to be an auntie, and with all that's been going on today, it's finally good to hear some exciting news. I got into a heated argument with Jacoby earlier, so I need to get out of here to see if he's made it home, okay?"

"Go handle your business. Thank you so much for everything, Kayla. I appreciate you more than you will ever know."

We hugged right at the door and then I left. I walked slowly to the elevator while punching Jacoby's number into my phone. It was almost seven o'clock. I wondered if he had made it home. He didn't answer his phone so I left a message, telling him to call me back. I was still looking down when the elevator opened. But when I looked up, Cedric was standing there with his hand in one pocket and his suit jacket was tossed over his shoulder. His stare was without a blink. So was mine.

"What are you doing here?" I questioned.

Cedric cleared his throat and swallowed. "I . . . uh . . . called Evelyn looking for you. She told me you were here. She didn't tell you?"

"No, she didn't."

"I'm not sure why, but after our conversation earlier, I came here to make sure you were okay."

I sighed from relief and smiled. "I'm fine. I feel a whole lot better, so let's go home."

I put my arms around Cedric's waist and rested my head against his chest. I asked how he'd gotten upstairs and he said he got on the elevator with a man who had a swipe card. The elevator took us back to the parking garage where we got in our cars and headed for home. I was glad to see Jacoby's car in the driveway, but when we went inside and Cedric tried to talk to him, Jacoby didn't want to hear it. He went into his bedroom and shut the door.

"I'm done," Cedric said, removing his clothes. "His ass will have to make the next move. I've had it with his disrespect."

"Don't give up on him just yet. He's going through a lot and we can't expect for this situation to change overnight."

"See what I mean?" Cedric went into the bathroom and turned on the shower. "You're always making excuses and taking up for him. I wish you would just say he's wrong and stop trying to sugarcoat shit."

"I admit it, okay. He's wrong. That's what our talk was about earlier. I told Jacoby to stop being so bitter and to put forth some effort to work this out with you."

Cedric didn't say anything. I watched as he lathered his body with soap, and it was one sexy sight to see water running from his body to the drain. I removed my clothes and stepped into the shower with him. We faced each other. The silence was broken when Cedric gripped my ass and inched me closer to him.

"I do love you, you know," he said. "In the midst of everything that is going on, you're still my wife and I appreciate you for being there for me."

"I love you too, and I certainly do my best to please you."

Our tongues danced through the falling water that ran from the showerhead and drenched us both. Cedric lifted and positioned me for more action against the wall. I held on to his neck and rubbed the back of his waves. During my orgasm, I dropped my head back as he sucked my chocolate nipples, trying to arouse me even more. Wanting to please him too, I released my legs from his waist and squatted in front of him. He pulled on my braids and pumped his steel deep down my throat. I massaged the muscles in his ass, and when they tightened, he pulled out of my mouth and resumed in my pussy where I needed to feel him the most.

Around midnight, Cedric and I were cuddling in bed. We had just finished another long, lovemaking session and were on our way to sleep. I couldn't stop thinking about Evelyn. I wondered if she had called Trina to tell her about the baby. I decided to check with Evelyn first, before I ran off at the mouth and said anything to Trina. I did, however, feel as though it wouldn't hurt anything if I mentioned it to Cedric.

"Guess what?" I said while rubbing the sparse, smooth hair on his chest.

"I know. You love me, right?"

I laughed and so did he. "Yeah, I do. A whole lot, but that's not what I was about to tell you. I was going to tell you that Evelyn is pregnant. I found out today and I'm so happy for her. You know she's always had a difficult time getting pregnant, and this is a huge surprise to all of us."

For a few seconds, Cedric didn't respond. I felt his body get real tense, so I looked up at him. A blank expression covered his face and I got no reaction from him.

"Did you hear what I said?" I asked.

"No, I—I didn't. What did you say?"

"I said that Evelyn is pregnant. What were you thinking about since you didn't hear me?"

"I was thinking about some stuff with Jacoby, that's all. I didn't mean to ignore you, but . . . uh . . . I guess that's good news. You know how wild she is. I assume she probably doesn't even know who the father is."

I frowned and playfully pushed Cedric's chest. "That's not nice. You seem to dislike my friends and you never have anything nice to say about them. Evelyn is not like that anymore and she has settled down a whole lot. Marc is the father, and from what she told me he's pretty excited about the baby."

"Yeah, well, good for them. Now, turn out the light on your side. It's already late and I need to get some sleep."

I reached over to the lamp to turn it off. I was ready for some more action, but Cedric had turned on his side to face the wall. He pulled the cover over him, and a few minutes later he was out. As for me, I couldn't sleep. I had too much on my mind, including my doctor's appointment tomorrow that was only a checkup.

Chapter Ten

Kayla

I hated going to the doctor's office, because no matter what I came here to do they were always busy. And then when they called my name to go back into one of the rooms, I still had to wait at least another thirty minutes to an hour to be seen. My doctor, Kenneth Woodrow, was a doctor I'd had for quite some time. And no matter how crowded his office was, I was comfortable with him and didn't want to switch doctors. The plus side was he was a fine black doctor who I trusted. I waited for him to come into the room, and sat on the examination table while paging through a magazine. The nurse had already taken a sample of my urine and she had drawn blood as well. I had on one of those ridiculous wrinkled gowns with an opening in the back.

I heard a knock on the door and Dr. Woodrow entered. Normally, he would be grinning from ear to ear, but I guess today was a hectic day for him.

"Hello, Kayla," he said, closing the door behind him. "How are you feeling?"

"I feel great. Just here for my regular checkup. I wanted to make sure everything is good with me."

Dr. Woodrow sucked his teeth and opened my folder to look at it. He nodded and scanned his eyes down the papers inside. He licked his lips then his brows shot up.

"It's that bad, huh?" I teased.

He finally smiled. "No, no. Not bad, but certainly not good, either."

My heart fell way below my stomach because I had no clue what he meant by that. "Not good? What's going on?"

Dr. Woodrow pulled up a stool and sat in front of me. "You know I don't like to get into your personal matters, but we've known each other for a long time. How has your marriage been doing?"

"It's been . . . been okay. I mean, Cedric and I have had some issues, but nothing that can't be worked out. Why are you asking—"

"Any issues with infidelity?"

I was straightforward with Dr. Woodrow and was a little irritated as well. "No. Not at all."

He scratched his head and glared at me. "You have chlamydia, Kayla. I suggest that you and your husband use condoms from now own because you don't want to open yourselves up to anything else."

My brows shot up; I was speechless. I had an out-of-body experience and I wasn't quite sure I had heard what he'd said. Chlamydia was something that young people—teenagers—got. Not a grown woman like me who was married and had been so for many, many years.

"Look, Dr. Woodrow, there has to be some kind of a mistake. Maybe my urine test got mixed in with someone else. I'm going to need for you to go back out there and clear this mess up."

"I understand that you don't want to accept this, but it's apparent that someone in the marriage has been unfaithful."

Hearing his comment made my blood boil. I knew darn well that it wasn't me and I suspected that it wasn't Cedric.

"No, you don't understand that we don't get down like that. Please go find out what the hell is going on and correct this mess, now!"

Dr. Woodrow stood up. He left the room and I hopped down from the examination table to put my clothes back on. If the organization in his office was this screwed up then I was going to have to find me another doctor. How dare he come in here feeding me this crap about having chlamydia? I was seriously considering a lawsuit against him for getting it wrong.

Once I put my clothes back on, I paced the floor and waited for Dr. Woodrow to return. My thoughts were all over the place. The what-if's started to kick in. My heart was already racing and when Dr. Woodrow came back into the room the same gloomy look was on his face.

"I wish I was wrong about this, Kayla, but I'm not." He handed me a piece of paper that showed the results to my test. He started to point out why he was correct, but I snatched the paper from his hand.

"This is such bullshit," I said as tears rushed to the brim of my eyes. "I don't believe this. Cedric would never—" I couldn't even finish my sentence because my gut had already told me what the hell was up. Jacoby had told me too, but I chose to accept what Cedric said as if his word was above all.

"I would like to give you a full examination, just to make sure everything else is okay with you," Dr. Woodrow said. "I want to check for herpes—"

I was so embarrassed that I ran out of the room in tears. Everybody was looking at me and questioning if everything was okay. I was numb all over. By the time I reached my car, I was a wreck. I felt like Dr. Woodrow had just told me I'd had cancer. The pain I felt from Cedric's betrayal was unbearable. I couldn't wait to confront him with this, and instead of waiting until he got home, I drove straight to his office. I didn't bother to clear up the smudged mascara that was running from my eyes, nor did I bother to straighten my clothes. My lips trembled as I stood at the receptionist's desk, asking where I could find my husband.

"He—he's in a meeting right now," the receptionist said with caution. "I'm sure he'll be done shortly, so why don't you have a seat and I'll tell him you're here."

"Don't bother."

I stormed off to the boardroom that was at the end of the hallway. The door was closed, but when I swung it open, Cedric sat at a shiny, mahogany wooden table with at least a dozen other executives in business suits. Many of them were chuckling until the door flew open and they saw me standing there, distraught. Shock covered their faces. The room was now so quiet that you could hear a pin drop.

Cedric shot up from the chair like a rocket, but by the time he could make it around the table I took off my shoe and flung it across the room, hitting him in the head. I then charged into the room with tightened fists. I swung out wildly at him and pounded his body with my fists so hard that he had to crouch down in the chair.

"You dirty, nasty-dick motherfucker! How dare you do this shit to me! How dare you give me a goddamn disease from one of your trifling whores!"

I didn't care about putting our business out there. I wanted Cedric to feel my pain and embarrassment too. My arms got tired from swinging, so I picked up the leather binder on the table and smacked him with it. Papers scattered everywhere and so did some of the men who were in the room.

"Call security," one of the executives said to another. "Hurry!"

With the crazed and disturbing look in my eyes, I was sure that they thought I was strapped. I wished I were, but unfortunately I wasn't. Cedric had finally stood up and tried to push me away from him.

"Chill the fuck out!" he shouted while shielding his face. "Stop acting a damn fool and get a grip of yourself!"

He locked his arms around my waist and squeezed so tightly that I couldn't breathe. I started pounding my fists at his back and a few minutes later two security guards rushed into the room. They pulled me away from him and locked my arms behind my back.

With a busted lip, Cedric plopped down in the chair and took several deep breaths. "Get her the fuck out of here. Call the police and have her arrested."

"You bastard!" I shouted and tried to spit on him. The security guards had to drag me out of the room, because I continued to charge at him and had fallen on my knees. I never, ever thought I was capable of getting my clown on like this, but I couldn't control my actions. Not until he was out of my sight.

Almost an hour later, the security guards released me and told me to leave the premises. I was also told to never come back. Apparently, they were following the orders of my husband, who had obviously changed his mind about having me arrested.

While in the car, I cried until I couldn't cry anymore. I called Dr. Woodrow to apologize for my behavior earlier. He told me that he wanted me to come back in for a full examination. He also said he would call in my prescription to the nearest Walgreens.

Yet again, I was humiliated as I stood at the pharmacy counter to pick up my medicine. There I was . . . walking around like a classy bitch with chlamydia. Pussy was all fucked up. There was no doubt that I was dying to get my hands on Cedric again. This mess was far from over.

I just didn't have time to deal with it tonight. So instead of going home, I called Trina to see if she was home. She wasn't there, so I contacted Evelyn. She answered and I asked her if I could stop by.

"Sure. I don't have any plans and I'll be here all evening," she said.

"I'm on my way."

When I arrived at Evelyn's place, she buzzed me right in. This time, it was me who needed comfort. I needed her to lend me an ear, give me some advice, and show me some support. But unfortunately, when I broke the news to Evelyn, she appeared just as taken aback as I was. Even her eyes filled with tears and she covered her mouth.

"You have got to be kidding me, Kayla. Wha—did—was the doctor sure about that?"

"Yes! Very sure. I've been walking my dumb tail around here in denial, dissing my son and believing every single lie that Cedric has told me. I feel like such a fool. I swear to God that I could kill him right about now."

Evelyn still didn't have much to say. She got up from the couch and went into the kitchen to get some water. She didn't even bother to offer me any, which wasn't surprising because I had obviously forgotten how selfish my best friend was at times. So selfish that I didn't feel at ease talking to her about this anymore.

I snatched up my purse, tucking it underneath my arm. "I'm going home to talk to Jacoby. I'll call you later."

Not saying another word, she walked me to the door and opened it. "I hope everything will be okay. That's a shame what Cedric did to you and he knows better."

I shrugged and moved forward to make my way to the elevator. Evelyn called my name and I swung around with anger displayed on my face.

"I don't mean to bring this up right now, but please don't forget about the money you promised me. I'm really in need, okay?"

Well, ain't that about a bitch? I was in need too, but she obviously didn't care. "Sure, Evelyn. I'll be sure to take care of that for you."

"Thanks."

I walked off and heard her close the door before I even made it to the elevator. Something was going on with her, but I didn't have time to worry about her, especially when I was trying to deal with all of this.

This time, I drove to Trina's place to see if I would get a different reaction from her. I felt down and out and needed somebody to be there for me. But as soon as I parked my car in a parking spot at Trina's apartment complex, I saw her sitting in the car with the pastor's wife, Cynthia. I was getting ready to get out of my car and go speak to her, but then I saw Cynthia lean in closer to Trina. It looked as if they were kissing. I squinted to get a closer look, noticing that they were.

I covered my mouth and sat still as if cement had been poured over me. I watched as the two of them laughed and kissed several more times before eventually getting out of the car and going inside. Several lights were on, but then they went out. I was sick to my stomach and wanted to throw up. Why in the hell was all of this coming down on me in one day? My best friend was a dyke? I couldn't believe it. And the pastor's wife . . . oh my, God! Really? What in the hell was going on? Why didn't I see the people in my life for who or what they really were? A dyke? Damn!

I refused to let Trina get away with lies, and what excuse could she come up with now? I felt so betrayed. The only time Trina was being truthful with me was when she wanted my money. Only then would she speak the truth. All of this other mess was a lie. She was living one big lie and had me believing that she and Keith were in love.

The wrinkles on my forehead deepened with every step that I took to her door. I banged on the door, knowing that she would do her best to avoid answering it. Little did she know, I wasn't going anywhere. I banged so loudly that one of her neighbors opened her door and went off.

"Damn, she's not in there. Come back next week or next year, and stop bangin' so hard before you wake up my son."

I ignored the black woman who needed to take her crusty-looking tail back inside and mind her own business. Today wasn't the day to mess with me. Little did she know, she was about to catch hell. I continued to bang on the door, but Trina didn't answer.

"I know you're in there, Trina!" I shouted. "Open the door!"

"Bitch," the neighbor hissed. "Did you hear anythang I just said to you? I got a baby in here tryin' to sleep. Unless you gon' brang yo' ass up in here and stay with him all night then I suggest you stop knockin' on her door like dat and take yo' uppity-ass back where you came from."

I turned and shot daggers at her with the look in my eyes. "Would you like to hear my suggestion to you? Take yo' ass back inside and put a plug in your freaking ears, bitch. If not that, go run some bathwater so you don't hear me knocking. You look like you could use a hot shower—and a lengthy one at that."

As soon as the woman stepped forward, Trina opened the door. She was wearing a purple silk robe and had on a pair of house shoes. Her short hair was messy and not a drop of makeup was on her face.

"What is going on out here?" she questioned. "Kayla, why are you out here banging on my door like you're Five-O?"

I folded my arms across my chest. "Because I would like to speak to you now, if you don't mind."

"Please let that bitch get whatever she gots on her chest off of it," the woman said.

"And please gift-wrap this bitch a dictionary, because she really needs one."

Trina pulled me inside and slammed the door. She turned on the light and stood looking at me like I was the crazy one. "What is it, Kayla? I was trying to get some rest. What is so important that you have to speak to me right now?"

"Don't play me like a fool, Trina. Where is she?"

Trina cocked her head back. "Where is who? What are you talking about?"

I figured she wouldn't be truthful with me. Hell, nobody was, so what did I expect? Instead of asking her again, I started to search her living-room closets.

"What are you doing?" Trina said, following behind me.

"I'm searching for the truth. That's what I'm doing."

"The truth about what?"

"You'll know when I find it."

I continued to walk around her apartment, searching every closet and looking underneath everything that I could see under.

"You need to leave, Kayla," Trina said. "Leave now or I'll have you arrested."

"Yeah, well, it won't be the first police threat of the day. Feel free to call whomever you wish to."

Trina stormed away from me and went into the other room. That was when I went into the bathroom and yanked the shower curtain aside. Inside stood Cynthia, covering her nakedness with a towel.

"I—I was just borrowing Trina's shower and—"

"Get out!" Trina said, pointing to the door. "How dare you come into my home as if you own it! Who in the hell do you think you are, Kayla? Who?"

I turned around and darted my finger at her. "I thought I was your best friend, Trina! The one who you share your freaking secrets with! The one who I could depend on when I needed you! The one who wouldn't lie to me about anything and the one person who I seriously thought I could trust! But who are you, Trina? Who in the hell are you, because you damn sure aren't my best friend!"

"I am that and then some! But—but I'm also gay!" Trina's voice softened. "I don't like men, but I do love women. So now you know, Kayla. Now . . . now you know my secret. So tell me. How does it feel to have a best friend who prefers to make love to women?"

I truly thought I was dreaming. God, please let me wake up from this dream and start this day all over again. But when I turned to look at Cynthia, it was all real. I looked at Trina and there she was staring at me, waiting for a response.

"You disgust me," I said, releasing deep breaths. "This is disgusting. How could you be over here having sex with the pastor's wife and then go to his church and call yourself a Christian? You're no friend of mine, Trina. I would be a fool to ever refer to you as one again. Don't you ever call me again, and as for you—" I turned to Cynthia. "You had better get on your knees and pray like hell for God to forgive you. What kind of woman are you? How dare you have others refer to you as the first lady of the church? How dare you?" I shouted.

I rushed out of the bathroom and bumped my shoulder with Trina's on the way out. She softly called my name, but I didn't bother to turn around. I got the hell out of there and drove to the nearest hotel so I could somehow or some way sort this mess out.

Chapter Eleven

Trina

I didn't feel so good after Kayla left. She didn't understand that this had nothing to do with her. It was more about not wanting anyone to know what was going on with me. I was so outdone that I made Cynthia put her clothes back on, and I asked her to leave. She, however, removed the towel from around her and straddled my lap as I sat in a chair.

"I'm not going anywhere and I'm here for you. Kayla is going to have to get over it. She has some nerves standing in judgment of us, and there are times when you can't help who you have feelings for. One day she'll understand. In the meantime, please don't let this stress you out."

"I can't help it. I feel bad for not being honest with her. I know that you'll be there for me, but I really need to be alone right now."

Cynthia removed herself from my lap and said nothing else as she got dressed. She kissed my cheek and headed for the door. "Hope to see you on Sunday," she said. "No matter what, we all still need Jesus."

She didn't lie about that, but hearing those words come from her kind of went in one ear and out the other. It was one thing to be gay, but then to be married and carrying on the way she was, wasn't right. I was participating in the mess too. I felt horrible for doing so. It was time to clean up the crap, but before I did anything I called Kayla to speak to her. She didn't answer so I left a message on her voice mail.

"I get that you're upset with me for not being honest with you, but please call me back so we can discuss this. I need to clear the air. After that, if you still don't wish to mend our friendship, so be it. At least hear me out and try to understand where I'm coming from."

I hung up and then called Evelyn to see if Kayla had called her. I hoped she hadn't, because I sure didn't want Evelyn to know my secret.

"She was over here earlier," Evelyn said. "But she left pretty upset about her and Cedric getting into it."

"About what this time? She needs to consider letting him go."

"Maybe this time she will. Apparently, he gave her a sexually transmitted disease. I'm not sure how he's going to explain that to her, but knowing him, he'll think of something."

"Are you serious?" I shouted. My heart went out to Kayla. Now I knew why she was so upset. Maybe this didn't have anything to do with me. She just caught me at a bad time. I was even more eager now to speak to her. "That's awful. Do you have any idea where she's at? I tried to reach her on her phone, but she didn't answer."

"I have no idea where she's at, but I'm not looking for her right now. I'm trying to find Cedric, the one who I would love to give a piece of my mind."

"I want to get at him too, especially for doing Kayla like that. She recommended that we stay out of her business, but this is downright ridiculous."

"Yeah, it is. But look. I gotta go. I need to get out of here for a while and I'm supposed to meet Marc for dinner."

"Maybe we can hook up on Sunday. I have information about a job you might be interested in, so I'll pass that on to you."

"Fine. I'll call you on Sunday and we'll go from there."

Evelyn hung up, but unlike her, I was very interested in where Kayla was. So interested that I put on my sweatpants and a hoodie, got in my car and drove to her house. Jacoby was there. He opened the door to invite me inside.

"Is your mother home yet," I asked.

"Nope."

"Do you know where she's at?"

"Yep."

"Do you mind telling me?"

"She asked me not to tell anyone."

"Jacoby, please. I need to see her and it is so urgent that I do."

As we stood in the foyer, we heard the garage door open. I rushed around the corner to see who it was, but it was Cedric. He looked at me and at Jacoby, who was standing behind me.

"What's going on?" he questioned. "What are you doing in my house?"

"I'm here looking for Kayla. Do you have any idea where she's at?"

"No, I don't. But you can stay here and wait for her, if you'd like to. I'm sure she'll be coming home soon; after all, where else is she going to go?"

I turned around to Jacoby and addressed him first. "Please forgive me for saying this and I truly mean no harm." I faced Cedric and pointed my finger near his face. "You are such an asshole. You're married to a beautiful woman and all you can do is figure out ways to treat her like shit. I look forward to the day when you have to bow down to her and beg for forgiveness. I pray that whenever that day comes, she'll spit in your face and have the guts to tell you to go to hell."

Cedric casually removed his jacket and started to unbutton his crisp white shirt. "Are you done? If so, you can get the fuck out of my house. If not, for the first time, my son will have to witness me kick a woman's ass like she stole something from me. But then again, you're not really all woman, are you? You like pussy too much to be a woman, and there is a possibility that you even love pussy more than me. So, man-to-man, mind your own business. Don't worry about Kayla, because at the end of the day, I got her back and front, not you."

Before I could open my mouth, Jacoby tugged on my arm. I turned around and he nudged his head toward the door. I hated to go there like this with Cedric. It took everything I had in me not to chew him up further. Jacoby walked away and I followed. As soon we went outside, he told me where Kayla was. I gave him a squeezing hug and drove to the Embassy Suites by the airport.

Jacoby told me Kayla was in room 324, so I went to that room and knocked. Kayla asked who I was, but fearing that she wouldn't open the door, I put my finger over the peephole and whispered "room service." She opened the door. When she saw that it was me, she walked away from it.

I went inside and stood in front of her as she sat on a couch with her hands covering her face. Her braids were in a ponytail, and she wore a long pajama shirt that was almost down to her knees.

"What do you want, Trina? Why are you here?"

"First, I want to say that I'm sorry about what has happened between you and Cedric. I'm not going to say anything negative about him, but please figure out a way to deal with him. He's out of control. As for our friendship, the only reason I didn't tell you about me being gay was because I knew you would react the exact same way that you did. I was afraid of losing our friendship, and my being gay has nothing to do with how I've treated you as a friend. I may have lied to you about this, but it was because of my own insecurities. I didn't want anybody to know, so please do not go around spreading my business to other people, including Evelyn. When I'm ready to tell her, I will. In the meantime, if you would prefer to end our friendship like this, I'll have to deal with it. It won't be the first time I lost those closest to me because of my preferences, and I'm sure it won't be the last. The choice is yours, Kayla. Just let me know what's up either way."

Kayla lifted her head and took a deep breath. She shook her head and her eyes searched me. "You know what, Trina? I do not have time for any of this. The only thing on my mind is what in the hell am I going to do about my marriage. Who you love or who you have sex with is not important to me. I don't have time to sit here and talk about this with you, but I will say this: I don't trust you and I never will. I thought I knew who you were, but I don't. I've shared some of my deepest secrets with you, yet you lied to me when I inquired about you being gay. I'm in a place where I don't want to be around anybody. So why don't you just leave and go be with whoever you want to be with. It doesn't mater how I feel about what you're doing—and why are you so adamant about seeking my approval?"

"I don't need your approval; after all, I am a grown woman who will make my own decisions. After what happened today, I felt obligated to come clean about my situation, so that's why I'm here."

Kayla's eyes grew wider. "Obligated? Girl, please. The only reason you came clean was because you got busted in the midst of screwing the first lady. Don't stand there like you came here to express all this crap to me because our friendship means so much to you. The bottom line is, if it did, you had years . . . plenty of years to tell me what was going on with you. I've been running around here with you, claiming you as my best friend and I really don't know much about you. How many other women are you screwing at our church? I'm sure they all probably think I'm some kind of gay trick too."

Kayla's harsh words stung. I looked at her and made myself clear. "This conversation is over. I tried to get at you like a for-real woman would, but I see that you're so fucking bitter at your husband right now that your mind is real twisted. I'm going to get out of here before I disrespect you, as you have clearly disrespected me. Have a nice life, Kayla. I'll be praying that everything works out for you."

I turned to walk toward the door.

"Don't pray for me, pray for yourself," she shouted. "Pray that you get your head on straight and that God can deliver you from being a lesbian."

Unfortunately, she touched a nerve. I turned around and let her have it. "I would rather be a lesbian any day of the week than be a dumb, disease-infected bitch who allows her husband to fuck all over her. Get your own house in order before you start running up in mine, trying to advise me on the best way to conduct myself. Good-bye, Kayla, and good riddance."

I walked out, telling myself that I would never, ever speak to her again.

Chapter Twelve

Evelyn

I called. He wouldn't answer. I left messages. He wouldn't respond. I didn't want to go to their house because Kayla was there, so the only place I could reach Cedric was at his office. I was pissed. After Kayla left my place and told me about the disease incident, I rushed to my doctor this morning, only for her to tell me the same thing. This fool had given me chlamydia and now he didn't have anything to say about it. I still hadn't had time to tell him about the baby either. There was so much mess going on, and Kayla had the nerve to be running around here looking for sympathy and wanting some attention. I was still waiting for her to swing some money my way. As of yet, she hadn't given me one dime.

I knew darn well where I could get some money from, and Cedric was a fool if he thought he was going to dismiss me. He didn't know who he was messing with. I wasn't a passive trick like his wife was. I thought he knew that, but maybe he needed to be reminded once again.

I entered the lobby with my dark shades on. My hair was pulled back into a thick, curly ponytail. My makeup was painted on like artwork and I was rocking some bright red lipstick that moistened my lips. The fitted sleeveless dress I wore appeared melted on my small curves, and I stepped like a model in my five-inch heels. I lowered my shades, peering over them to look at the blonde-haired receptionist who always had an attitude.

"Would you let Cedric Thompson know that his baby's mama is here to see him?"

The receptionist's eyes grew wide. She picked up the phone and buzzed Cedric on speakerphone. "Excuse me, Mr. Thompson. A woman is here to see you. Is it okay for me to send her to your office?"

"What woman? Is it my wife? If so, you need to call security."

"No, it's not your wife. But the woman says that she's your . . . uh . . . baby's mama."

Cedric paused then told the receptionist to buzz the door and let me through. I hadn't noticed the door before. Obviously, it was something new. I swished my hips from side to side as I made my way to Cedric's office. The door was wide open, and when I walked inside he was gazing out of the window with his hands in his pockets. He looked dynamite in a brown tailored suit, but too darn bad his dick was shooting fire.

"Close my door," he said without looking in my direction. I closed the door then proceeded forward and removed my glasses.

"I guess you already know that you're on my shit list and why, right?" I said.

"I don't give a damn about your shit list. And just so you know, you're on mine too."

I folded my arms across my chest. "For what? Please tell me why my name would be on your list then I'll tell you a gazillion reasons why yours is on mine."

Cedric turned to face me. His eyes scanned me up and down, before he walked up to me and stood within inches. "Because you're a fucking slut, that's why. And if you came here to tell me about your baby, I don't want to hear about it. Tell Marc to step up and be a man. I hope he's capable of providing for you, and all I can say is the two of you deserve each other."

He came off as a little jealous, causing me to reach out and slap his ass. He caught my hand in midair. He shoved me backward and I stumbled. "Don't bring that bullshit in here today, woman! I'm not in the mood! Since we're done talking, you can get the fuck out of here. Don't come back unless I invite you to."

I was very disturbed by Cedric's tone and his actions. He was showing his ass, but I wouldn't dare let him see how hurt I was by what he'd said.

"When all is said and done, this child is yours and you know it. Marc doesn't have to step up because, eventually, you'll have to do it. In a big way, I may add, so prepare yourself to deal with it. And one more thing before I go. No, two more things: Spreading diseases around town ain't really cool, and that nasty dick of yours will never get to touch this pussy again. If you even think about making things hard for me, I will go to your wife and tell her everything I know. I will make your life miserable, Cedric, so you'd better think long and hard about how you intend to play your hand going forward. Meanwhile, I'm broke. I need some money. I hope you don't mind kicking me out a little something, especially after all I've done for you."

Cedric leaned against his desk with a sly smirk on his face. "You're a real piece of work, Evelyn, and I finally get why I started fucking with you. I got a couple of things to add before you go too, so listen up real good because I'm not going to repeat myself again. You can tell Kayla whatever it is that you want to. I don't give a fuck, and our marriage has been over with for quite some time. Whatever you tell her won't matter to me not one bit. The baby, mine or not, will be better off aborted. Besides, I don't have kids with whores and I will never take care of a child who belongs to one.

"Finally, pertaining to your little situation with chla-mydia, why are you and Kayla running up in here like the

sky is falling and it's a big deal? Go pop some damn pills
to clear that shit up and be done with it. It's not the end of
the world and some people get caught slipping from time
to time. I could tell something wasn't right with that other
pussy when I was in it, and believe me when I say I feel
awful for making you swallow, and, uh—well, you know
what freaky you did. Anyway, forgive me. When we both
get cleared up, maybe you'll have a change of heart and
let me hit it again. Call me when you're ready. You know
where to find me."

Cedric winked and walked around his desk. He picked
up his phone, holding it in his hand. "Work without play
is no good. I'm done playing, so now I need to get back to
work. Get the fuck out of my office. If I have to listen to
one more word from you, I'll have you removed from this
building."

Okay. So I thought I was a bad bitch, but Cedric had
the last word. As soon as I opened my mouth, security
came and escorted me out. I still had so much to get off
my chest, but it wasn't getting off anytime soon. I had
to rethink my approach to this situation. It started with
going to see Kayla so I could see where things between
her and Cedric now stood.

I swerved in and out of traffic while trying to reach
Kayla on my cell phone. I hadn't spoken to her since she'd
left my place the other day. Whenever I called her home
phone, Jacoby told me she wasn't there. I wondered if
Trina knew where she was, but when I questioned her she
had an attitude.

"No, I don't know her whereabouts, and quite frankly,
I don't care."

"Since when? Have the two of you had some differences
again?"

"Yes we have. This time, however, I don't think we're
going to be able to repair our friendship. Kayla said some

things to me that I didn't appreciate, so I'm going to leave her alone and let her do her."

"How many times have the two of you been down this road before? Y'all always make up and you know she's dealing with some crazy stuff right now. I don't get why you're tripping. We've been up and down throughout our friendship, and the least you can do is try to understand her situation and be there for her."

I was feeding Trina a bunch of bull. I liked when her and Kayla were at each other's throats. It was kind of hilarious to me, and they always tried to get me to pick sides.

"I hear what you're saying, but it's not like you've actually been there for her either, have you? Every time I talk to you, you're too busy and you don't seem to have time for me or Kayla."

"I have my own problems to deal with, Trina. You know I still haven't found a job and I'm looking forward to meeting with you so I can hear about that lead you mentioned. And I also didn't tell you this yet, but I'm pregnant. That's why I've been acting so standoffish. I have a lot of things on my mind, okay?"

"I'm surprised to hear you're pregnant. Congratulations to you. Do you know who the father is?"

"Hell, yes, I know who the father is. Why would you ask me that? Like . . . like I'm some type of confused whore who's been sleeping around with a bunch of men."

"I didn't mean it like that, but you have talked about several men that you've been seeing. Plus . . ." Trina paused for a few seconds. "Never mind. I got this lady over here who wants to buy some artwork. I'll call you later, all right?"

"Yeah, whatever, Trina. I wish you would be clear about what you want to say and stop beating around the bush."

"I don't want to assume anything and hurt your feelings. I could be wrong about this, but tell me the truth and be honest. Have you been having sex with Cedric?"

I didn't dare respond yet. I wanted to tell Trina what I had been doing, but now wasn't the right time. "I don't know where you're getting your information from, but I am highly offended by you asking me that. What kind of person do you think I am, Trina? I would never stoop low like that and have sex with my best friend's husband. Are you crazy for asking me something like that?"

"Maybe I am, but like I said, I gotta go."

She hung up on me. I couldn't help but to wonder where she had gotten her information from. I assumed that nobody knew about me and Cedric but us. I guessed Trina had been speculating, but she was definitely on to something.

Kayla had been missing in action, but while Cedric's foolish self was still at work I drove by their house to see if she was there. She wasn't, but Jacoby was outside washing his car. The music was blasting and he had on a pair of sagging jeans that showed his drawers. A wife-beater displayed the muscles in his arms, but there weren't many muscles to get me hyped. Jacoby was thin and very tall. He was a handsome young man, and I couldn't help but sit in my car for a few minutes, thinking if I wanted to include him in my next plan. I put my shades back on and got out of my car. I swayed my hips, locking his attention as he kept his eyes on me.

"Hi, Jacoby. I've been trying to reach your mother. Do you know where she is?"

"Yep," he said, then bent over to swirl the soapy rag on his car.

"Do you have any idea when she's coming home?"

"No, I don't."

I sighed, because I didn't appreciate how short he was with me. "Listen. I know she probably told you not to let anyone disturb her, but she needs us right now. The last thing Kayla needs is to be cooped up somewhere without family and friends. I would like to see her. Therefore, I would appreciate if you would tell me where I can find my best friend."

"Sorry, but I have specific rules to follow, and I'm going to follow them. All I can say is she checked out of one hotel and is now in another one."

"Which one, is the question. Please tell me."

Jacoby shook his head, signaling no. He continued to wash around his car, then he headed inside with several dirty rags in his hands. I followed behind him, still trying to persuade him to tell me where Kayla was.

"Jacoby, why are you ignoring me? You know how close your mother and me are. Don't you know that she needs me? What if she's suicidal and needs somebody to talk to? I'm sure you know the condition she's in, especially if you've been speaking to her."

Jacoby tossed the dirty rags in the trash can, and then he looked underneath the sink and got a few more clean ones. He held them in his hand and turned to face me. "I have been speaking to her every day. And you know what, Evelyn? She sounds like she's doing okay. All she needed to do was get away from my father for a while. Maybe she'll be able to rethink some things and do what is right for her future."

"Lord knows I hope you're right. She has gotten herself in a real big mess and this doesn't look like it's going to be an easy fix."

Jacoby shrugged as if he didn't care. He stood silent for a minute. His eyes narrowed like Cedric's often did sometimes. I stepped up closer to Jacoby, leaving very little breathing room in between us.

"You know what," I said in a soft tone. "You're looking more and more like your father every day. You had better be careful with that, because that would put you in a position to have any and everything you could possibly want."

Jacoby displayed a smug look on his face, identical to Cedric. "So, let me get this straight. You're saying that I have it going on just like my father does? Really?"

"You sure do. And let me repeat myself again: That means you can have anything you want. All you have to do is ask for it."

Jacoby inched forward, this time leaving no space between us. My breasts were pressed against his chest. I could feel his muscle swelling against me. Our eyes stayed locked together, and I was surprised when he slipped his arm around my waist.

"Anything," he said in a whisper.

I nodded and confirmed my words. "Anything. Especially for a young man who wears a size thirteen shoe."

"Fourteen," Jacoby said, while lifting me on the island. He parted my legs then moved in between them. The direction of his eyes dropped to my lips and mine dropped to his. I reached out to grab the back of his head, but as I leaned in to seal a kiss, he backed his head up.

"I—I can't help but to think about what positions I would like to put you in, Evelyn, but maybe I should let you decide."

Jacoby reached into his pocket and pulled out his cell phone. He turned it so I could see the pictures, and to my surprise, there were pictures of Cedric having sex with other women.

"What about that position?" Jacoby said, flipping through the pictures. "That's a good one right there. Or how about this one?"

My face was already cracked and had hit the floor. I looked at the picture of Cedric and me having sex. It was in his bedroom when Kayla was away in Atlanta.

"I say we go upstairs to my parents' bedroom and get busy. What say you?"

I jumped down from the island to gather myself. Jacoby was playing games with me and I certainly didn't appreciate it. "I say, you can take all of those pictures and shove them. I don't know what kind of game you're playing, but you're way out of your league."

I tried to move, but he remained in front of me. "I think I'm playing this game quite well for my age, and even though I may be my father's son, I don't want anything to do with his whores. What may be good for him is not good enough for me. So all I'm going to ask you to do is get the hell out of my mother's house and please figure out a way to check yourself on the major disrespect."

I was highly upset by the way he spoke to me, but he would never know it. I switched to my game face and displayed a smile.

"You mean, *your father's house*, because your mother's name is not even on it. And at least we agree that I have been good to your father. Sometimes, leftovers are. You can't knock it if you haven't tried it—and with that, I'm on my way home. If your mother calls, please tell her to reach out to me. And if you by chance have a change of heart about me, my door is always open."

Jacoby didn't respond. He just stared at me. That was when the smirk appeared and something eerie was trapped in his eyes. "How's the job coming along, Evelyn? You've been rather busy. I wondered if you were able to find another job yet."

"Why are you concerned about my job? I see your mother has been over here running her mouth again."

"No, honestly, she hasn't. I heard about your troubles through someone else. It's a shame what happened to you on your job and I hope you're about to find another one."

Jacoby walked off, leaving me puzzled about how he knew so much. First, the pictures of me and Cedric alarmed me. Then, with him bringing up my job, something wasn't adding up with this.

"Are you the one responsible for what happened on my job?" I asked.

Jacoby snickered and slapped the rag against his hand. "Ding-ding. I guess you are somewhat bright after all. It took you a minute, but you finally got it. You didn't think I was going to stand by and let you make me and my mother's life miserable, without you suffering any consequences, did you? And trust me when I say this is just the beginning, especially if you don't do the right thing and end your friendship with my mother and stop fucking my dad. I know it's going to be difficult for you to tear yourself away from him, but believe me when I say he's no good for you. You deserve better, Evelyn. I do mean that from the bottom of my heart."

Jacoby opened the door to go back outside, but I rushed after him. This conniving fool had cost me my damn job and I was anxious to hear about his plans to destroy me. Prior to today, he was the least of my worries. Now all of that had changed. I still had something up my sleeve, though, and I was ready to pull it out like a weapon and use it.

I ran in front of Jacoby, stopping him dead in his tracks. I pointed my finger in his face and spoke through gritted teeth. "You listen to me, boy. If I find out that you had anything to do with me losing my job, you're going to be in big trouble. As far as Cedric is concerned, you don't have what it takes to be like him. The reason why you can't get along with him is because you're jealous. You wish that his blood ran through your veins, but your blood comes from a lowlife negro who isn't shit. So the next time you speak to your precious mother, be sure to inquire about your father. The question you may want to ask her is, which one is he?"

I stormed away, mad as hell. How dare this kid try to mess with me? After my conversation with Cedric, I'd just about had it with these people. Kayla and her entire family could go to hell. I was over this bullshit, and I had to figure out another way to get my hands on some money.

Chapter Thirteen

Kayla

Jacoby had been blowing up my phone, telling me to come home. I rushed out of the Renaissance Hotel, and as soon as I walked through the door, he was sitting on the couch in the living room, waiting for me. His eyes were puffy; he was roughly massaging his hands together. Fearing that something bad had happened, I hurried into the room and stood in front of him.

"No more bad news, please," I said tearfully. "What's going on now?"

Jacoby looked up at me. A tear sped down his face and dripped on his trembling knee. "I got a question for you," he said. "And please do not lie to me, Mother. I want the truth."

My stomach was already being squeezed in a tight knot. There was only one thing that could make Jacoby this upset. I hoped my secret was not about to come out.

"What is it?" I said softly.

"Who is my damn father? Is Cedric not my real father?"

"Absolutely, hell fucking no, I'm not," Cedric said from behind me.

I swung around and staggered as I saw him standing there. "It's time to come clean and get all of this shit out in the open. I'm glad you finally asked the question, Jacoby, and for a long time I was very confused myself. I was suckered into believing that your mother really and truly loved me, but then I discovered that it was all a lie. She used me, man, so that she could have all of this. She lied to you, for the sake of keeping her financial situation on lock. Then she turned around and made me out to be the villain in all of this. I'm just a monster that she created. There was no way for me to stay committed to a woman who hurt me as much as she did. I hope you see now, son, why I've conducted myself in such a horrible manner. Maybe I was wrong for taking some of this out on you, and all I can do is ask for your forgiveness."

My mouth hung wide open. Cedric was so good at manipulating people. I prayed that Jacoby wouldn't fall for the bullshit. But when I turned my head to look at him, the anger in his eyes had deepened. His stare was cold. He didn't dare take his eyes off me. I stood there, unprepared. I didn't know what to say, and I wasn't even sure if the truth was good enough.

"Do not believe that mess Cedric just told you. This has nothing to do with my financial situation and—"

"To hell with your financial situation!" Jacoby yelled. "Who in the fuck is my father?"

My whole body shivered from his tone. No matter how upset he was, he needed to calm down. "Don't raise your voice at me. I'll tell you who your father is, but we need to go somewhere away from Cedric—"

"Stop beating around the damn bush," Cedric said. "Tell Jacoby who his father is right now. As a matter of fact, fuck it. I'll tell him. His name is Arnez Jackson and he was one of my friends in college. He started doing some crazy shit, got himself in a whole lot of trouble, dropped out of school, and got on drugs. He came to me about three years ago, asking for some money and threatened to tell you that he was your biological father, if I didn't give the money to him. I didn't give him a damn dime, but someone else paid him a large sum of money to keep his mouth shut. I don't have to tell you who that person is. I'll just say that you're looking right at her."

I could barely breathe right now. I held my chest and looked at Jacoby with sorrow and much regret in my eyes. "I lied to protect you," I confessed. "Arnez had disappointed me so much and I wanted you to be raised by a man who I thought you could look up to and who could show you how to be a real man. I failed you, son. I'm so sorry for—"

Jacoby hopped up from the couch. He spoke through gritted teeth while looking at me and Cedric both. "Sorry my ass, Mother. I can't believe how pathetic the two of you are. I have wasted too much of my time, trying to get the two of you to act like grown people who should know better. Is it so damn hard to love and respect each other? Is it so easy to keep secrets from the ones you love? No wonder I've been running around here feeling as if I don't fit in. Cedric not being my biological father explains a lot, especially his ill treatment and his I-don't-give-a-fuck attitude. I can't say that I blame him, Mother. Only because you created this mess. I don't give a damn how you get out of it, but whatever you do, leave me the fuck alone. I'm done."

Jacoby rushed past me, and when I grabbed his arm he shoved me backward, almost knocking me on my ass. Cedric jumped in front of him, holding his shoulders and looking directly into his eyes.

"From the bottom of my heart, you will always be my son. I regret that it has come to this, but I'm delighted that the truth has finally come to the light. Take all the time you need to let this soak in. If you need me, I'll be right here."

Jacoby didn't respond. He opened the front door and left. I didn't bother to go after him, only because I knew he wasn't prepared to listen to my explanation for all of this. Cedric had definitely gotten what he wanted. I was anxious to wash that smug look off his face.

I smacked away several tears and was seething with anger as I spoke to him.

"If you knew about Arnez, why didn't you ever say anything to me? You know darn well that the only reason I didn't come clean about this was because of the kind of man Arnez was. You were broke back then, Cedric. My decision didn't have anything to do with money and you know it!"

"Yes it did, so wipe your tears, cut the drama, and stop acting. That's all I talked to you about—my plans to be wealthy. You knew I had everything lined up, and you had just as much faith as I did that we would one day have all of this and then some. The bottom line is you lied to Jacoby and you lied to me. Face it and stop trying to justify your actions. From day one I knew Jacoby wasn't my son. When I looked into his eyes all I saw was Arnez. But I went along with it, because at the time I did love you. For years, I had to live with your fucking lie and pretend that everything was all good. Now, you want to come down on me for the shit that I've been doing. You want to run up in my office, kick my ass, embarrass the hell out of me, and pretend that you've been the good wife. You can't pretend anymore, Kay. The shit has hit the fan. I expect for you to be out of my house and out of my life for good. My divorce lawyers will be in touch soon."

This time Cedric walked away. I had to admit that I was unprepared for all of this. I feared what was about to happen and it wasn't like I had anyone in my corner. The only person I was somewhat on good terms with was Evelyn. Maybe I could stay in one of her extra bedrooms for a few weeks, until I worked this out. I had to settle things down, get to my bank account and clear it out fast. I didn't have money to waste at hotel rooms and I knew

Cedric was about to shut my life down. I had to admit my mistakes. Maybe I did break Cedric's heart. Maybe he was the kind of man he was because of me. The least I could do was apologize.

I walked slowly up the stairs and into our bedroom. Cedric was in the sitting area with his feet propped on the table in front of him. His hands were locked behind his head and he looked to be in deep thought.

"I don't even know if I should be apologizing or if I should be demanding an apology from you." I walked further into the room and stood by the fireplace. "We've both made some mistakes and you have no right to point the finger at me. In my heart, I still believe that we can somehow work things out. The last thing I want is a divorce. You say that you don't care anymore, but that's because you're angry right now. I will give you all the time you need to think this through, but please do not go rushing off to divorce me."

Funny. Just yesterday I couldn't wait to file for a divorce. I had an appointment scheduled with my lawyer and everything. Today was a new day. I still wondered if my actions had hurt him as much as he proclaimed they did.

Cedric lowered his arms to his elbows and licked his lips. "The damage is already done, Kay. I'm no good and I'll never be any good. You hurt me too bad and unfortunately, I'm not as forgiving as you are. Don't waste your time fighting for something that will never be. I assure you that this marriage will never be what you expect it to be, because the truth is, I don't love you anymore."

His words cut deep. I stood, feeling as if a sharp knife had been stabbed in my stomach. I wanted to drop to my knees as Cedric left the bedroom. And when I heard the door open and his car speed away, I cried my heart out. My husband and son were gone. I had no clue how to piece this all back together. I basically had to start all over, but I didn't know where to start. I was confused. Not in a million years did I see this day coming.

The next day, which was Saturday, I went to the bank to withdraw my money. Unfortunately for me, Cedric had transferred all of my money into another account. He was unaware of a small savings account I had for Jacoby that had almost ten grand in it. I took that money out, but I had to be very careful how I spent it. Basically, I had to make it stretch until I could find a way to stabilize my situation.

Once I left the bank, I checked out of the pricey room at the hotel and drove to Evelyn's place with my luggage in tow. I had plans to go back home and remove some of my expensive jewelry, but I was so sure that Cedric had changed the locks already.

A woman was going up on the elevator, so I got on and took it up to Evelyn's floor. When I knocked on the door, she opened it with a bowl of ice cream in her hand and a spoon was in her mouth. She glanced at my luggage and then she widened the door for me to come in.

"I need a place to stay," I said immediately. "Do you mind if I stay in one of your rooms until I can figure out what to do about my situation?"

"I've been trying to find out exactly what is going on with your situation, but you've made yourself unavailable."

"I know. I needed some time alone to think."

I rolled my luggage into the living room and left it there. I plopped down on the couch, along with Evelyn. I told her everything that had happened between me, Jacoby, and Cedric. I also told her about my fallout with Trina, but I didn't mention that Trina was gay. I worked around that little situation, feeling that if Trina wanted Evelyn to know she would tell her.

"Wow, Kayla, I—I really don't know what to say. I'm surprised that you never thought Jacoby would find out who his real father was, and I'm more in awe to know that Cedric knew about it all this time and didn't say anything."

"Not one word. He put me on the spot, and Jacoby now thinks that I'm the worst person on this earth."

"I doubt that he thinks that, and like you said, he just needs time. As far as Cedric is concerned, I don't know what to say about him. It sounds like the marriage is over. Maybe it's a good thing that you're moving on."

"I never said anything about moving on. I intend to save my marriage and my family will not be torn apart because of this. I've been trying to put myself in Cedric's shoes, and a part of me understands where he's coming from. My lies may, indeed, have hurt him. It explains why he's changed so much over the years."

Evelyn rolled her eyes and threw her hand back. "Girl, please. Cedric is faking the funk. He's making excuses for his actions and is trying to justify why he's been an unfaithful husband. I don't know why you don't see that. It's part of his plan to make you feel like you're the one who has done wrong, when realistically it's him."

"I thought about that too, but there is no denying that I lied to him, Evelyn. And this wasn't just any ol' lie either. It was a lie that I knew would affect us deeply, so here we are."

"So, I guess you've forgiven him for the whole chlamydia thing, huh? It's okay that he's been having sex with other women, and you're perfectly fine with him taking the money out of the bank and changing the locks on the doors. And then the way Cedric told Jacoby that he wasn't his father was okay with you too. Forgive me for not understanding your feelings about this. I'm seriously over here scratching my head."

"You wouldn't understand any of this, because you're not Jacoby's mother and you're not the one married to Cedric. You didn't witness the hurt in their eyes. I did. You don't know how much damage my lie has done to them. I do. Like Cedric said, some people just aren't as forgiving and they have their own way of dealing with things. Of course I'm upset about the chlamydia thing. I'm upset about the other women as well, but I have bigger fish to fry than to worry about hoes out here screwing my husband."

Evelyn pursed her lips and got off the couch. She put her empty ice cream bowl in the sink then she opened the fridge to get a bottled water. "Would you like something to drink? All I have is water, nothing else."

"No, I'm fine. I haven't forgotten about giving you the money I told you I would give you, but things have changed and I'm unable to help you out like I said I would. Right now, I have about ten grand to my name. The only thing I can afford is about fifty or sixty bucks to help you get some groceries. I'll be able to give you a few extra dollars for letting me stay in your room, but to be honest, Evelyn, I may need the money that I have to fight Cedric in court. I have a feeling that he's not going to back down and he's planning to leave me high and dry."

"Possibly, but here's the problem that I have. Marc is supposed to be moving in with me on Monday. He's supposed to help me with my finances, so I can't let you stay here. It wouldn't look right, but had you come to me sooner, maybe I could have made some different arrangements."

After all that I had done for her, I couldn't believe what she'd just said. "I won't be in the way. I only need to stay here for—"

"No," Evelyn said adamantly. "You *would* be in the way and I don't want Marc to be uncomfortable. He already gave me first month's rent, so I'm not going to renege on him."

I was in total disbelief. The expression on my face showed it. "I could stay on the couch and make sure I'm gone all day. Marc wouldn't even know I lived here and—"

"No, Kayla, that wouldn't work."

The tone of my voice rose. "So what do you want me to do, Evelyn? Sleep in my car?"

"Why not? It's big enough, but I doubt that you'll have to do that. Why don't you go make up with Trina? She has an extra bedroom, doesn't she? It's unfortunate that I can't help. Whether you know it or not, I'm deeply sorry that I can't."

This conversation with Evelyn left me speechless. In order for me not to cuss her out, I got off the couch, grabbed my luggage, and decided to go. I didn't even say good-bye. I proceeded to the door and didn't bother to close it after I walked out.

Chapter Fourteen

Trina

Whenever I was under pressure I threw myself into work. I had been trying to avoid too many people and it had been a minute since I had worked from the office. I suspected that Keith was eager to finish what we never got started and he'd still been trying to contact me.

Cynthia had also been ringing my phone, but I wanted to keep my distance from her. I avoided church altogether. When she came to my apartment last night I didn't answer the door. Lexi hadn't been bugging me as much, but she did call last night to inquire about my sudden distance. She said that she would stop by today to see me and when I heard a knock on the door, I was so sure that it was her. I looked through the peephole and saw Kayla standing there with her head lowered. I wasn't up to arguing with her, so I ignored her.

"Trina, I already heard you walking to the door. I came here to apologize and to ask you a few things. Please open the door."

For whatever reason, I couldn't stay mad at Kayla if I tried. Ever since we were in elementary school, I always managed to forgive her for all of the hiccups in our friendship along the way. Yes, we'd said some harsh things to each other over the years, we'd done some ugly things, and we'd kept many secrets from each other. But at the end of the day, I still cared for her. I still considered her my best friend—one that I was mad at but still loved with all my heart.

I opened the door, but refused to smile at her, even though I wanted to. She had a weary look on her face and was dressed in a pair of stonewashed jeans and a T-shirt. Her braids were wrapped in a bun and her gold hoop earrings matched her thong sandals.

"Apology accepted," I said to her and said no more.

Tears welled in Kayla's eyes and she reached out to embrace me. She wasn't what I considered an emotional woman, and whenever she cried I knew something deep was going on inside of her. "I'm so sorry for what I said to you," she said. "I—I don't know what got into me and I never should have treated you that way."

Seeing her cry made me cry, but I hurried to blink away my tears. "I'm sorry too. I was wrong for saying what I said to you as well. I knew you were going through some things and I apologize for not understanding your situation."

We backed away from each other. I invited her to come in and follow me. I went into my studio to finish painting, and she sat on one of the stools watching me.

"By the look in your eyes," I said, "I can tell there has been a lot going on. I'm all ears, so tell me what's been up."

Kayla told me about the situation with her family, and then she told me about Evelyn. I just shook my head, but deep down I knew the real reason why Evelyn had been acting funny. She had been fucking around with Cedric and she was also pregnant with his child. I wanted so badly to tell Kayla the truth, but she was already on the brink of losing it. I didn't want to cause her more pain. I felt horrible about not saying anything, and there I was—again—feeling as if I was betraying her. Thing is, I wasn't sure if it was my place to say anything. I didn't want to be the one to open up another can of worms, and I thought about what this would do to my friendship with Evelyn. We still got along well, but there was no secret that Kayla and I were closer. It had been that way for quite some time, only because Kayla had always been there for me, way more than Evelyn had been.

"So, that about sums up my drama," Kayla said. "And with that, I need a place to stay. I won't wear out my welcome and I will do my best to be out of here in a few weeks, no later than a month."

"It doesn't matter how long you stay. You're welcome to my guest room. But I have to say this to you, and I don't want to make you feel uncomfortable about this. My life goes on over here. I have several lady friends who come to see me from time to time and I'm not going to change my situation because you don't approve of it."

"Look. You do you and don't worry about how I feel. I doubt that I ever will approve, but so what, Trina. It has a lot to do about how I was raised and I can't change my way of thinking overnight."

"I get that and it's cool. All I ask is that you refrain from any negativity about my situation while you're here and please do not insult my guests. It's already hard enough being me. The last thing I need is a friend who constantly judges me."

Kayla told me that she understood. She went to her car to get her luggage and when she came back in she put her luggage in the guest room. She watched me paint for a while and complimented the work I had done.

"You have some serious talent," she said. "I'm surprised you don't have your own studio. You really should try to open up a store or something."

"What do you think I've been trying to do? It's kind of hard when you don't have money to do those things. If I had your money, I could've made big things happen by now."

Kayla dropped her head and looked down at the floor. "Tell me something, Trina. Have I been a good friend to you? Do you think I helped you enough, considering all of the money I was sitting on?"

I put my paintbrush down and wiped my dirty hands on my sweats. "Our friendship hasn't been all about what you can do for me, but it has been about what we can do for each other. It's my responsibility to make things happen for myself, not yours. There are times when I wanted to ask you for the money to help me get my business started, but this is something that I want to do for myself. If you had offered, of course I would have taken the money, but I'm glad you never did."

Kayla got up from the chair and walked over to the window to look out. "If the shoe was on the other foot, I would've wanted you to help me. I mean, that's what friends are for too, and it's kind of like a blessing that I could have passed on to others. Maybe that's why I'm in the situation I'm in right now. You have to admit that I've been a little selfish. Maybe that's why Evelyn has her issues with me, and I can honestly say that I kind of get her coldness at times."

"Okay. So you are a little selfish, but we do have to take responsibility for our own lives. I said it and now you know. Now if you don't mind, I would like to get out of here and go get something to eat. I'm starving and I'm not going to stay cooped up in here all night."

"Food, here we come," Kayla said.

Before we left, I called Lexi to see if she would meet us at Louie's in the Central West End. Kayla called to see if she could reach Jacoby. A sad expression was on her face and she told me that his number had been disconnected.

"I'm going to drive by the house to see if he's there," she said. "Afterward, I'll meet you at the restaurant, okay?"

"That's fine. Be careful and don't push so hard, Kayla. Eventually, he'll come around."

"I hope so."

Kayla left in her car and I got in mine, heading to the Central West End. It was warm outside, so I wore a pair of baggy jeans shorts and a half top that showed my midriff and tattoos. The shorts hung low enough where my belly ring showed and my preppy tennis shoes provided a casual look I was trying to accomplish. When I got to Louie's, I was seated at a booth in the far corner. It was packed and the music in the background was rocking. Flat-screen TV's were mounted on the walls and several people were there to watch the basketball play-offs.

I sat for at least thirty minutes, wondering where Lexi and Kayla were. But when I looked up and saw Keith, I put the menu up to cover my face. Unfortunately, he spotted me before I could hide myself.

"Trina, is that you?" he asked as he walked up to me with one of his friends next to him.

I lowered the menu and smiled. "Hey, Keith. What's up?"

"Nothing much. This is my boy, Dane. Dane, this is Trina. The amazing, beautiful woman I was telling you about."

"Oh, yeah," Dane said, extending his hand. "Nice to meet you."

"Same here."

"So . . . uh . . . are you here with someone?" Keith asked.

"A couple of my girlfriends will be here shortly—and as a matter of fact, here comes one now."

I saw Kayla coming my way. It didn't appear that she had any luck with Jacoby. I introduced her again to Keith then to Dane.

"Hello," she said, keeping it short, and then she took a seat next to me. "Why don't the two of you join us? I'm sure we can all fit in this booth, can't we?"

I didn't necessarily approve of Kayla asking them to sit with us and I wasn't so sure how Lexi would feel about it. Either way, they sat at the booth with us and everybody started ordering drinks and food. Minutes later, Lexi strutted in. She had a thing where she always wanted me to herself, so she was surprised to see the others sitting at the booth with us. I introduced her to everyone. Keith and Dane didn't know what was up, but Kayla appeared to be uncomfortable.

"I want to sit next to Trina," Lexi said.

In order for that to happen, Kayla had to move. She looked at me and I didn't say one word. In an effort not to make a scene, I hoped she would just get up and allow Lexi to sit where she wished. Thankfully, Kayla did.

"I'm sorry I'm so late, but I got held up at the nail shop. Trina, do you like my nails?"

"They're nice. Real nice, but why don't you go ahead and order your food? Everyone else has already ordered theirs."

Lexi picked up the menu, looking at it. Dane and Keith were talking and checking out the game and Kayla sat on the end stiff as a board. She kept looking around the restaurant at several gay people, and her eyes bugged when she saw two men kissing. Her nose winced at two ladies who stood by the bar with their hands in each other's pockets, but I did notice her smile at a man who waved at her from afar. When he walked away, she was back to looking stiff. Her arms were so tight against her and she made sure that Lexi didn't touch her. Lexi gave the waitress her order and then passed her the menu. As we all began to talk, Lexi placed her hand on my leg and started to rub it.

"I can't believe I finally met you," Dane said to me. "All my boy ever talk about is you. You got this fool feeling some kind of way about you."

Kayla smiled, but Lexi narrowed her eyes then rolled them. She squeezed my thigh then took my hand and put in on her lap. From underneath the table, she inched my hand up her skirt, trying to get me to feel her hot spot. I saw Kayla observing from the corner of her eye. She then picked up the glass of water in front of her, gulping it down.

"Yeah, Keith and I are good friends," I stressed. "It's good to know that he still has nice things to say about me."

"Always," Keith said, putting his cute dimples on display. "But I'm not letting you get away from me tonight. So you may have to say bye-bye to your girlfriends and come spend some quiet time with me."

Lexi pinched my thigh real hard and snapped her head to look at me. I mean, What in the hell did she want me to say? I wasn't about to put my business out there tonight, so I ignored her gestures that were very annoying; so annoying that Kayla stood up and tucked her purse underneath her arm.

"I'm not hungry anymore," she said. "I need some fresh air and I think I'm going to get out of here and go home. It was nice meeting you all. Trina, can I have the keys to your apartment? I will see you later."

I gave Kayla the keys and she walked off. Lexi questioned why Trina was going to my apartment and, not satisfied with my answer, she pouted. Keith kept pursuing me and Lexi was upset that I hadn't told him to back off.

"You invited me here," she said with an attitude. "But it's obvious that you don't have time for me tonight."

Lexi stormed off, leaving me in a position where I had to explain my silly friends. "I apologize, but I have friends who demand my attention. Don't take them walking out like that personal. I'm sure I'll catch up with them later."

Keith and Dane looked at each other then shrugged. They continued to watch the game and get their drink on. I did as well. I had a good time with the fellas and when we got ready to go, Keith reminded me about his invitation.

"Just for an hour or so," he pleaded. "I live nearby and you don't have to travel far."

I kept telling myself that I didn't want to be alone with Keith, but I also didn't want to go home and face Kayla, nor did I want to hear Lexi gripe about tonight. Therefore, I decided to take Keith up on his offer. Dane left in his car and I followed Keith to his house.

It was an old, historic house that had been remodeled in the inside. I loved how spacious it was and the old wooden staircase and the stained-glass windows revealed the real history behind the house. Keith showed me around, leaving me in awe. The ceilings were very high, and every single room had an old fireplace that Keith said dated back to the early 1900s.

"When I updated the place there were some things that I didn't want to change. There's a lot of history in the house and I've even been told that there are ghosts living here."

"Yeah right," I said, walking closely behind him. "I find it hard to believe that you live here all alone."

"My grandparents used to live here, but when they died they left the place to me. I had a roommate a while back, but he started stealing shit so I had to put him out. Ever since then, I've stayed here by myself. I'm hoping to one day raise a family up in here . . . have a wife and some kids, and do that happily-ever-after stuff."

Well, he was barking up the wrong tree with me. I didn't want any children and I surely wasn't trying to be nobody's wife. I kept my mouth shut, until he walked me into another spacious room on the third floor that was his studio. His beautiful artwork was all over the room. I was left breathless. I only wished that I had a place like this to do my work.

"Believe it or not," he said, "this used to be a ballroom. You see how high the ceiling is?"

I nodded and gazed up at the cathedral ceiling that was painted gold. Crown molding surrounded the room and the silk curtains that draped the windows made this one classy room.

"I can picture a ballroom being in here. And with all of this space you must be in heaven. Why do you even need the space at work?"

"I just go there when I get sick of being in here. It can get kind of boring at times, and it does me good to get out."

Keith began to show me some of his paintings, and he also showed me some of the invoices he'd gotten from orders. I wished I had it going on like him. Dude was straight-up making a for-real living off of his talents.

"I'll be glad when I get to your level. I mean, my work is good too, you know?"

"Very good," he complimented. "I've seen a lot of it, but it's nowhere near better than mine."

We laughed, and I had to admit that he was way more skilled than I was. I began to look through more of his paintings and as I browsed the room, he dimmed the lights. I turned around and Keith walked up to me. He eased his arms around my waist and pulled my body closer to his. Needless to say, I was real nervous because in that moment, I was forced to admit that I had some feelings for him.

"Do you have any idea how long I've waited to get you alone like this?" he asked.

"I do, but I'm not sure if I'm ready for this right now."

"Why not?"

I looked into his eyes that were so sexy and luring. "Because, I'm so unsure about a lot of things."

"I can tell and I have an idea what things you're speaking of. Just give me a chance, and whichever way you decide to swing with this relationship is fine with me."

I released a deep breath that caused my breasts to rise against his chest. He leaned in to kiss me and the moment our lips touched I was eager to get out of my clothes. I started to remove my shorts, but Keith stopped me by touching my hand.

"Wait a minute. I want to do this right. Give me a minute."

Keith walked away then pulled an old-fashioned, velvet-covered chair that I'd seen in one of his paintings, to the middle of the floor. He kept his eyes on me as he removed his clothes then he sat in the chair. On display was the beauty of his nakedness and those colorful tats that made him look like a work of art sitting there. I watched his dick grow from six inches to about a strong eleven. I was impressed.

"Okay, now it's your turn. But remove your clothes in an artistic way while I sit here and stroke my brush."

Keith held his dick and began to slow-stroke it with his hands. I wasn't sure how artistic I could get with removing my clothes, but I did so by going real slow and creating a small pile beside me. Keith's eyes were locked on my small breasts and then the direction of his eyes lowered to my shaved pussy that was already leaking. I rubbed my hands all over my naked body, and when I turned around he had a view of my picture-perfect ass that I was proud of. I squeezed my ass cheeks then I bent far over to entice him even more. With my head dropped, I looked between my legs. Keith gestured his finger in a come-here motion.

"Now all you have to do is back up to me. Don't turn around just yet."

I backed up and as he held his dick straight up, I held onto the arms of the chair and eased down on his hard muscle. It put a large gab between my pussy lips and I certainly could not take it all in at once. I worked with the tip first and as my insides moistened more, I was able to glide up and down on Keith's muscle with ease. He planted soft, delicate kisses against my back and stroked me at a smooth pace that made me hear music in my head, even though there was none.

"Now tell me," he whispered between the kisses he planted on my back, "how does that feel?"

I shut my eyes and poked out my breasts to form an arch in my back. I slowly grinded my hips to the music playing in my head, yet was unable to spill my guts and tell him how him being inside of me made me feel.

He lifted his hands to squeeze my breasts and with his lips, hands and muscle in action at the same time, I couldn't hold back my inner thoughts much longer. I revealed them in a soft whisper. "You feel damn good, Keith. Too good."

"So do you."

He released his hands from my breasts and lowered his fingers to my clitoris. He swiped it delicately like a paintbrush and the vibrations of his fingers caused me to gasp and widen my eyes. I squeezed his wrist, trying to calm the intensity of how he was making my whole body quiver.

"Let it go, baby," he said. "Get it all out and don't hold back on me."

I let the deep breath that I was holding escape from my mouth and released my hand from his wrist. His fingers moved faster over my clit and his tool was so far up in me that it brushed against every inch of my walls. Seconds later a flood of my juices drenched his vibrating fingers. I cried out "*Keeeeeith*" and bent over to drop my face in my hand. My emotions ran high because I didn't want this to feel so spectacular. I told myself that a man wasn't capable of pleasing me, but there I was, wanting more of Keith. I wanted him to stay inside of me, and when he lifted me up by my waist and tried to pull out of me I rejected his move.

"What are you doing?" I asked. "Stay there. I'm not finished."

"Neither am I."

Keith stood me up straight and got behind me. He turned me around and sat me in the chair. He then spread my legs, placing each of them on the arms of the chair. With my pussy in his view, he kneeled between my legs and leaned in to suck my breasts. His mouth was massaging them so well that the arch in my back formed again. I could feel heat from my mouth that stayed open, to the tips of my toes that were curled. Keith continued to massage my breasts, but now with his hands. A trail of his kisses flowed down my stomach, into my pieced navel, and landed right at my pussy. He pressed his thick lips against mine and used the tip of his curled tongue to separate my slit. With ease, he brushed again and again.

With a little force from his tongue, he sucked and fucked me to a new level. With his vibrations, he broke me down and made me cum all over his handsome face. I squirmed in the chair, causing it to tilt backward, but then Keith caught me. He lifted me and secured my legs around his waist. I loved a strong man and that he was. Eager to feel him, I was the one to put him back inside of me. But all he did was stand still and hold me up. He searched into my eyes that were filled with many questions that only I could answer.

"What?" he said. "Tell me what's wrong."

My eyes watered because I was so confused. I thought I was done with men, especially after my first love, BJ, had done me so wrong. He beat me and dared me to tell anyone. He threatened to kill me, and raped me whenever I told him I didn't want to have sex. I hated him so much that I told myself that if love ever presented itself again, that love would be for another woman. Especially after my ex went to jail, I continued to pursue women. Now things had changed. I didn't know what I wanted going forward, but for right now, I wanted Keith.

"Nothing," I said after a hard swallow.

"Tell me," he repeated. "I want to know what you're thinking."

Silence soaked the room. I squeezed my arms around his neck and placed my lips close to his ear. "I—I'm thinking that I'm gay and—"

"No, you're not. Confused, unsure, hurt . . . but definitely not gay."

"How can you be so sure that I'm not?"

"Because . . ." Keith squatted and laid me back on the floor. "Because if you were gay, your pussy wouldn't be able to react to me the way it just did, your body wouldn't tremble like it has done all night, and if a woman was truly who you wanted to be with then you would totally reject me. There's still time to do it, and all you have to do is walk out that door and leave."

I replied to him by turning on my stomach and backing my ass up to him. He was crazy if he thought I was going to depart from this—there wasn't a chance in hell that I would. We displayed our artistic talents to each other for the next few hours, and I'll be damned if I didn't leave his house the next morning feeling like a brand-new woman.

Chapter Fifteen

Kayla

I had a difficult time sleeping last night. I left the guest room and went to go watch TV in the living room. That was where I fell asleep on the couch, hoping that Trina would come in and wake me. But by six o'clock in the morning, she still wasn't home. I assumed she was with Lexi. I was thankful that they hadn't come back here to finish up what had gotten started at the restaurant. Seeing what I saw made me very uncomfortable. I had a hard time accepting Trina's status and I felt kind of bad for walking out of the restaurant last night. But her girl Lexi was working me. She was so needy and she irritated the hell out of me. Surely Trina could do better and as far as I could see it, she had made some really bad choices with women.

Keith, however, was a different story. He was an extremely attractive man, but Trina didn't seem to be giving him much play. That was her loss because I would take him any day over that Lexi chick and Cynthia.

Thinking about my bad choices with men and about how much I didn't have much room to talk, I got up to take a shower. Like the rest of Trina's place, the bathroom was very colorful. Pink, yellow, green, and purple daisies accessorized the bathroom, and they were on the shower curtain and wallpaper too. The colors were a bit much for my taste, but all I needed right now was water.

While in the shower, I pondered my situation. I called Jacoby again and called home, but that number had been disconnected too. I was very worried about him, but as with anything, I suspected it would take time to heal. I had to give him space and not force this issue with him. But this was hard. Harder than I ever thought it would be. I even wanted to reach out to Cedric again, but I changed my mind about doing that. For now, I decided to wait. Wait and see what the next move would be, good or bad.

After my shower, I went to the bedroom and changed into a comfortable silk nightgown that went all the way down to my ankles. I wasn't going anywhere today and the plan was for me to relax. I went into the kitchen to cook breakfast. When I glanced at the clock it was almost nine o'clock. Just as I got ready to call Trina, she came through the door. The look of *I just had sex* was written all over her face and her smile on display said it all. I could only imagine what probably happened between her and Lexi. I quickly washed the thoughts from my head.

"Good morning," she said with much pep in her step. She walked up to me in the kitchen and gave me a hug.

"What's this for?" I said, hugging her back.

"No reason. Just for being you."

Trina kept smiling as she headed down the hallway. She went into her bedroom then came out with clothes to take a shower.

"I'll take some sausage and eggs too. Burn my toast a little and kill it with strawberry jelly."

I shook my head and got busy with breakfast. By the time Trina came out of the bathroom, breakfast was on the table. I poured orange juice in two glasses, but Trina reached for a bottle of Ciroc vodka.

"You couldn't be serious," I said. "This early, Trina?"

"Yes. Now pass me the glass of orange juice. I need something strong this morning."

I gave her the glass and she filled it to the rim with vodka. We then blessed the food and sat at the table to eat.

"I guess I don't have to ask why you're just now coming in, do I?" I said, prying.

"No, Mother, you don't. But I will say that I had a very interesting night and a pretty interesting morning too."

"You don't have to tell me. It's written all over your face. And if being with Lexi makes you this happy, who am I to judge? I want to apologize for running out of the restaurant like I did last night. This may take me some time to get used to, but at the end of the day, you're still my best friend and I love you."

"*Awww*," Trina teased. "That's so sweet. I love you too, bestie, and I do understand how you feel about my relationships. But just so you know, Lexi is not responsible for this smile you see on my face this morning. Keith is."

I rolled my eyes and pursed my lips. "Whatever. You played that trick on me before, Trina. Told me how much you were feeling Keith and you weren't even thinking about him. That's too bad, because he is gorgeous. I don't like my men that dark, but I could see myself getting it in with a man like that."

"Yeah, well, you're not the only one, and I'm not lying to you this time. We got it in last night, and when I say we got it in, I really, really mean that he got it in there. *Waaaay* in there."

We laughed and I didn't know whether to believe her or not. "I don't believe you. You had me convinced that you were done with men, and now you're telling me that you spent the night with Keith. I think you're just saying that because you know how I feel."

"Truthfully, I don't care how you feel. And I'm telling you that Keith and I had amazing sex last night. We topped it off with more sex this morning. He took me to a level up here." Trina raised her hand up high to show me. "And I'm so high right now that I can't come down."

I looked at her from across the table, trying to feel her out. It didn't appear that she was lying to me, and when her cell phone rang, she smiled and hit the speakerphone.

"Hello," she said.

"Didn't I tell you to call and let me know you made it home?" Keith said.

"I was getting ready to do that. You called when I had my hand on the phone."

"I'm not buying it, but I'm glad you made it home. I had a great time last night and this morning. I'm looking forward to seeing you again real soon, but you make the call, all right?"

"Will do, and I will do so real soon. Enjoy your day and thanks for calling."

Trina punched the button to end the call. She looked at me and shrugged. "Now what? I told you I was with him, didn't I?"

"That just about confirms it, but here's what I want to know: What are you going to do about that obsessive chick who couldn't keep her hands off you? I'm sorry to say this, but she was working the heck out of me. I believe in love and everything, but she was showing too much love. And does Keith know what's—"

"Yes, he knows. He also knows how I feel about him, so I have some serious thinking to do. Lexi has been there for me for a long time. The last thing I want to do is hurt her feelings. She does have some growing up to do, but I like her."

"What about Cynthia? Have you seen or spoken to her?"

"I have, but she's back on her husband's team right now. She does that from time to time, so our relationship really isn't a consistent one. My biggest problem is Lexi.

From the way I feel about Keith right now, she's bound to get hurt."

"Yes. And learn from me . . . do not hold back the truth from anyone. Once you feel sure about your feelings, tell Keith and Lexi what's up."

"I plan to. But I need to be sure about who I am and what I want."

Trina sipped from her glass then squeezed her eyes and rubbed her throat to soothe the burn. She bit into her toast and picked at the cheese eggs with a fork.

"Tell me something, Trina. How long have you known you were like this? I mean, you did a hell of a job hiding this from me and Evelyn, unless she knows too and hasn't said anything to me."

"No, she doesn't know. And what's so funny is I actually had a crush on her for a long time. I still think she got it going on, but there is much about Evelyn that turns me off too."

I was surprised to hear Trina confess her feelings for her. That made me a little tense. I tried not to interrupt and say the wrong thing. "I don't necessarily see that as a funny thing, and to me it sounds kind of weird. Did you ever act on those feelings and since you're being honest, did you ever feel that way about me?"

I could tell that my questions were making her uncomfortable, but I did want to know.

"Slow it down with your questions and let me finish what I was saying. I used to have a crush on Evelyn, but I don't anymore. I think you're a beautiful woman, but because I knew you were committed to Cedric, I never really thought about hooking up with you. I've been like this since me and BJ parted ways. What I never told anyone was that he beat me, raped me, treated me like shit, and threatened to kill me many times. If you remember, during that time I became distant with everyone. I told y'all everything was good, but it wasn't. Those black eyes you saw me with were not from car accidents or from me falling. When I broke my arm that time, I wasn't injured at the gym. BJ did all of that to me, and had he not gone to jail, I know he would've killed me. After that, I was done with men. I wanted no parts of them, so I started dating women and felt as if I could relate better to them."

I laid my fork down and wiped my mouth with a napkin. "I feel so terrible about this, because deep down I knew BJ had been abusing you. I never said one word to you, nor did I encourage you to leave him or go get help. I guess I was so wrapped up in my own—"

"Regardless, I wouldn't have listened to anything you said. There was nothing you could've done, so don't go blaming yourself. All I ask is that you keep what I've said to you this morning between us. I don't want Evelyn to know any of this, because that girl is the walking *National Enquirer* and she would put my business out there."

We laughed because Trina had spoken the truth. There was always one friend in the bunch who was out of control.

"I won't say a word, but what I would like to do is change the subject. I want to hear more about your time with Keith, and please tell me when you plan to hook up with him again."

Trina gave me explicit details of what transpired with her and Keith yesterday. I was blushing and shaking my head. I was so excited that I had to get me a drink too. We took the conversation over to the couch, laughing our asses off.

The conversation about Keith made me think of Cedric. He had always been a great lover and still was. But maybe that part of my life was over. I didn't know, but either way, today felt good. I got blasted with Trina. It had been a long time since we'd had such a fine time.

"You should not drink anything else," Trina said, snatching the glass from my hand. I had spilled some of the alcohol on the floor and she stumbled to the kitchen to empty my glass.

"I do—don't need anything else to drink," I slurred and wobbled as I stood up. "A—and neither do you!"

Trina turned up a bottle of Hennessy while standing in the kitchen. I shook my head and plopped down on the couch. "Call that bitch Evelyn over here so I can give that heefer a piece of my mind for dissing me," I said.

"It's *heifer*, not *heefer* and I'ma call her over here so the two of y'all can make up. Where . . . where my phone at?"

Trina slammed the Hennessy bottle on the counter and patted the pockets on her sweatpants. She stumbled back to the couch and fell back on it, next to me. She punched in Evelyn's number and a few seconds later she answered.

"Say bitch," Trina slurred. "Get on some clothes and come over here right now."

"Who is this?" Evelyn snapped.

We giggled and that was when I cleared my throat and yelled into the phone. "It's Big Daddy calling. Get over here now or else yo' ass is grass. I don't want no back talk, woman, ya hear me?"

"Trina and Kayla, stop playing. What is wrong with y'all this morning? Are the two of you drunk?"

Trina looked at me and held her hand in front of her mouth. "*Daaaamn*, are you drunk? I know I'm not, so she must be thanking that we—"

"I'm thinking that y'all are drunk and how pathetic that must be, especially since it's this early on a Sunday morning. What about church? Are either of you going?"

I slapped my leg and cracked up. "*Noooooo*, no church for me this morning, no siree. But I will be there next Sunday for sure."

"I see the two of you need a good old-fashioned cussing out. I'm on my way and y'all better have y'all's act together when I get there."

Trina tossed the phone on the floor and by the time Evelyn got there, we were acting like complete fools. The music was blasting and Trina was walking around like a chicken, flapping her arms and poking her neck out. Evelyn and I nearly died from laughing. It felt really good to have this much fun with my best friends. We still had issues, but the truth was . . . what frenemies didn't?

Chapter Sixteen

Evelyn

I was exhausted. Being with Trina and Kayla wore me out, and I was glad to get out of my place. I had been worrying myself sick about everything. The baby was on my mind and at this point, I wasn't sure if I should have it or not.

Yeah, it was my best friend's husband's baby, but so what? It wasn't like I tried to get pregnant by him. It just happened and I was left trying to figure this mess out by myself. There was no way in hell I wanted Kayla to stay here and I was delighted to see that Trina had let Kayla stay with her. That way, I didn't feel so bad about lying to her about Marc. The truth was, I hadn't seen him since we had left dinner that Sunday. He pissed me off by tossing so many compliments Kayla's way, and I viewed it as complete disrespect. He didn't even say anything nice about me like I had asked him to, and all he had done was embarrass me that day.

I so badly needed a drink, but because of the baby I didn't drink anything while I was at Trina's place. I had cut back on smoking too; didn't want to bring more problems to myself than I'd already had.

The day had come and gone. I had a job interview in the morning. Trina had given me the information about a secretarial position in Clayton. I wasn't interested in that position, so as soon as I hit the door, I threw the paper she gave me in the trash. I thought about my previous job, and when I thought about the possibility of Jacoby somehow sabotaging me, I realized that if he did, he probably did me a favor. I wanted out of that place and I got tired of kissing my boss's ass. By the way he treated me I should've been out of there. If Jacoby thought he had hurt me, he was sadly mistaken. He actually did me a favor, so that case was closed.

My interview tomorrow was for another customer service position. I liked working the phones and it always kept me busy. Hopefully, I'd get the job, and wanting to be well rested and ready to go in the morning, I shut it down right before ten o'clock. With my peach bra and panties on, I cuddled with the warm blanket and pulled it over my head. My eyes fluttered and I felt myself entering a deep sleep. What seemed like hours later, I felt something crawling on my leg. I kicked whatever it was with my feet and when I snatched the blanket away from my face, I looked up and saw Cedric standing at the end of my bed, scrolling the tips of his fingers against my leg. He was dressed in a suit, but his jacket and shirt were unbuttoned.

"What are you doing here?" I moved my legs to avoid his touch.

He snatched the blanket off me and tossed it on the floor. Without saying a word, he crawled on the bed and got on top of me. I resisted by trying to push him away, but he pinned my hands to the bed and maneuvered his body in between my legs. His lips touched the side of my neck and he pecked down it.

"Stop this," I said through gritted teeth. "I don't want you anymore, Cedric! Get up and get out of here. Now!"

He ignored my order and continued to peck down my neck. He started to grind his package between my legs and the harder it got, the more I resisted.

"No!" I shouted. "*Stooooop! Pleaaaase, stop!*"

Cedric halted his kisses and looked into my watery eyes. "You know this feel good to you, so quit pretending. I came here to tell you that it's over between me and Kayla. I filed for a divorce today and whether you wanted me to do that or not, it's done." He pecked my neck a few more times then stopped. "I—I've had time to think about how wrong I was about you and my baby. I'm excited about being a father. With Kayla out of the way, the two of us can be together. We can be good parents to our baby and you can let me take care of you like I want to. It's over, baby. I hope like hell that you're glad it's over."

I was speechless. I took several deep breaths and they slowed with every word that he spoke. Was it really over? Was it now my time to shine? I didn't quite know what to say, but the resisting stopped. My legs fell further apart and when Cedric released my hands, I used them to pull his shirt and jacket away from his chest. Without removing his pants, he unzipped them and stretched the crotch section of my panties over to the side. After putting on a condom, his dick filled me up. While he pushed deep strokes into me, I lowered my hands down into his pants and gripped his ass. My nails sunk into his flesh and I sucked his lips with mine.

"I'm so glad that Daddy's home," I said between sloppy, wet kisses. "I'm . . . so . . . glad . . . you're . . . home . . ."

"Me too."

Cedric tore into me like a maniac that night. He didn't leave until noon, causing me to miss my interview. Truthfully, I didn't even care. I had Cedric back on my team, and when I checked my account the money had been flowing again. I smiled and fell back on my bed, screaming "Yes!"

Later that day, I got a call from Trina that came from out of the blue.

"I need to speak to you as soon as possible. It's very important, Evelyn, and I can't go another day without getting this off my chest."

I wasn't sure if Cedric was coming back today or not, but I told Trina that we could meet. She wanted to meet at a downtown bar and grill that we used to meet at, but I thought that was odd because she knew I couldn't drink. I still agreed to it, and as soon as I put on some clothes I left.

When I arrived at the bar and grill, Trina was sitting at a booth in a pink-and-black sweat suit. There weren't too many customers inside and the lighting was so dim that I could barely see her. I made my way over to the booth, but immediately noticed the blank expression on her face when she saw me.

"I suspect this isn't going to be good by the look on your face." I eased into the booth and set my shades on the table.

"Unfortunately, it's not going to be, especially if what I suspect is going on winds up being the truth."

I had a feeling where Trina was going with this, but the first thing I needed was a cold soda. I flagged down the heavyset waitress with dirty-blond hair and asked her to bring me one. I then opened my clutch purse and pulled out my compact mirror. I dabbed my lips with red lipstick then smacked them together.

"Okay, Trina, go. The floor is yours and I'm all ears."

She didn't beat around the bush. "Are you having sex with Cedric and is that his baby you're carrying? I want the truth, Evelyn, and I want you to tell me now."

I folded my arms across my chest, as if I were offended. "I don't know why you keep confronting me with this dumb shit, but to answer your question again, no. No, I'm not having sex with Cedric and I'm not having his baby. I told you that I was pregnant by Marc and we are still seeing each other."

Trina glared at me and sighed. The waitress brought my soda over to the table and asked if I wanted anything to eat. "We got hot wings, hamburgers, hot dogs—you name it, we got it," she said, smacking on gum.

"No, thank you. The soda will be fine."

The waitress looked at Trina. "What about you, cookie? Can I get you anything other than the milkshake you're drinking on?"

"Not right now. If I need anything else, I'll let you know."

"Okay," she said, then squinted to get a closer look at Trina. "Say, anybody ever tell you that you look like that chick from Destiny's Child? You know the brown one with the cute tush and not that Beyoncé."

"Who Kelly? Kelly Rowland?" Trina questioned.

"Yeah, Kelly. I like her a lot."

"No, that's the first time I heard that, but thanks for the compliment."

"No problem," she said, and then looked me over. "You gals are really pretty. Your hair looks curly like Beyoncé, but you're much prettier than she is. I guess you can tell that I'm really not a fan and the way my husband looks at that woman pisses me off. I know I got lots of weight to lose before I can look like she does, but I'm slowly working on it."

There was no doubt that the waitress was working my nerves, but she was helping me get my thoughts together, now that I knew what this conversation would be about.

"Well, good luck and don't be too upset," Trina said. "Beyoncé would probably die to have your crystal-blue eyes and so would I."

"Really?" The waitress smiled harder and showed her stained teeth. Yucky, I thought. Her eyes weren't really all that, either.

"Thank you, but I'm not going to keep disrupting you two. Enjoy y'all's day and holler if you need anything."

She walked away and Trina picked up where we left off. "Marc, huh," she said. "Well, I need to let you in on something right now. I saw Marc at the grocery store last week. We talked and he said that he hadn't heard from you. When I mentioned a baby, he damn near fell on his ass because he hadn't a clue what I was talking about. So either he's lying or you're lying. I have a strong feeling that it's you."

I cut my eyes at Trina and looked away, thinking hard if I should tell her the truth. Eventually, I expected it to come out and if Cedric and I were planning to be together then maybe it was time to admit to the breaking news.

"Yes. Yes, I have been seeing Cedric and I am pregnant with his child. The last thing I ever wanted to do was hurt Kayla, but she has always had certain things that I wanted and desired to have for myself."

Trina had a look on her face that could kill. You would have thought that I just told her it was her husband. I didn't understand why she thought any of this was her business to begin with.

"I don't know if I should reach across this table and smack the shit out of you or if I should feel sorry for you. I can't believe that you have that much jealousy in your heart for Kayla—and for God's sake, Evelyn, she is supposed to be your best friend. What are you thinking?"

"You want to know what I'm thinking? Well, what I'm thinking is that Kayla may have been a good friend to you, but she hasn't been one to me. She knows—and has known for quite some time—how messed up my situation is, but all she does is sit back on her millions and get a kick out of me begging her for money. She shops at Saks while we shop at Target. She pretends like she doesn't know what's going on in our lives, and the first thing she always says is,

'Why didn't you tell me you needed something?' Why tell someone who already knows? If she really cared about us, she would offer to help us."

"Evelyn, you need to get it through your thick head that Kayla doesn't owe us anything. And please tell me what your messed-up financial situation has to do with your decision to fuck around with her husband? I'm not making the connection here. What you're saying sounds like a bunch of bullshit."

"Bullshit or not, it's the truth. If I had her money, you would be set. You would have everything you ever wanted and so would she. We've been friends for a long time. Shared our lifelong dreams, talked about our futures, and prayed for doors to open for all of us. They opened for her, but she never looked back. You can't deny that, Trina, and now that her world has come crumbling down, she has to come to us for help. I just couldn't find it in my heart to help her."

"Okay, fine, that's how you feel. But tell me again where Cedric comes into all of this. He's a lowlife bastard. I swear if I ever get some alone time with him, I could just . . . just kill him."

"Violence won't solve anything and you need to stop poking your nose where it doesn't belong. Cedric is my ticket to get out of the rut I'm in. He's been giving me money from time to time, but I'm so far in debt that it may take a while for me to get out of it. I didn't plan to get pregnant with his child, but it happened. All I can do is take this opportunity and run with it."

"Opportunity? You really see this as an opportunity?"

"Yes, I do. An opportunity to have some of the things in life that I've never had. For once, I just want a taste of the good life. I want to shop until I drop. I want to drive in fancy cars and live in a house like the one Kayla lives—or should I say, *lived in*. I want to know for a fact that the electric company can't turn off my lights, and I want to travel the world and see more than just the end of my street."

"You can have all of that one day, but this is not the way. Cedric is not going to be your ticket to anywhere but hell. Look at what he's doing to Kayla right now. She depended on him to take care of her and stick by her side, for better or worse. Now, she has to figure out a way to make it on her own. You can't trust a man like him and having his baby is not going to save you."

"It may or may not, but it's a start. I don't trust Cedric, but I'm going to milk him for every dime that I can, while I can do it. During the process, some people's feelings may get hurt and some things may have to come to the light. Meanwhile, I have to see about me. I need to take care of me and my child, and at any cost I will do it."

Trina rubbed her forehead and squeezed it. "If you've been feeling like this, why don't you tell Kayla? As long as we've been friends, you owe that to her. While she may have done some things that you disagree with, you should have gone to her and said something about how you felt. This is so awful, Evelyn, and I don't think you realize how much damage this is going to cost all of us."

"If you want her to know, and if you're so worried about damaging your friendship with her, then you tell her. You consider yourself a true friend, so tell me, Trina: What's holding you back and keeping you from saying anything?"

"Because, it's not my place to say anything. I feel as though I'm caught in the middle."

"I'm giving you permission to get out of the middle. I won't feel betrayed if you tell her about this and it's just a matter of time before she finds out. Cedric has filed for divorce. I suspect that things are about to change real soon."

"Meaning? Are you planning to marry him or something? Is it really that serious?"

"Not hardly. But we will be spending more time together. At my place, as well as at his."

Trina's phone rang and when she looked down at it she decided not to answer. "I can't take any more of this right now. I don't know what I'm going to do, but all I can say to you right now is that you're wrong, Evelyn. So wrong for all of this. You have shown me what kind of friend you really are and this shit is scary."

"A good friend to friends who are good to me."

Trina didn't bother to reply. She left five dollars on the table and walked out. After she left, I reached for my cell phone to call Marc. I was ready to chew him out for talking to Trina, but I was startled when he said he hadn't seen or spoken to her.

"I don't know why she would lie on me like that, but either way, I need to call you back. I'm busy right now," he said.

I hung up and sucked my teeth as I thought about that lying bitch. She found out what she wanted. The question was, what was she going to do with the information?

Chapter Seventeen

Kayla

I was still feeling hung over from Sunday and it was Tuesday. Trina called last night and told me that she was spending the night with Keith. I hoped that she wasn't staying away from her apartment because I was here. The last thing that I wanted was to inconvenience her. I called her cell phone to check on her, but she didn't answer. As I was leaving her a message, a call interrupted. It was coming from an unknown number.

"Hello," I said.

"I want to meet my real father," Jacoby said. "Can you pull some more of your tricks to make that happen?"

I wanted to go off on him for speaking to me that way, but I had waited so long for him to call me that I didn't want to blow it. "I don't do tricks, but I can see what I can do to make that happen. Where are you?"

"I'm at Adrianne's house right now."

"How have you been?"

"Just fine, Mother. Perfectly fine and I couldn't be better."

His voice was filled with sarcasm and I hated it. "Have you been to school?"

"Of course."

"Have you been staying at home?"

"Yes, I have, but I've also been in and out. I'm trying to keep busy, but the thoughts of my father keep bugging me."

"I know and I get it. I take full responsibility for what I've done and I didn't want to hurt you like this. You have to believe me when I say that. It pains me that you believed what Cedric—"

"I couldn't care less about Cedric. All I want to do is look my real father in the eyes. I want to talk to him and possibly get to know him. You denied me that opportunity. I'm so angry with you for doing this."

"Fine. Then allow me to make this right. Give me a number where I can reach you and I'll call you back as soon as I reach him."

Jacoby gave me a number where I could reach him and hung up. My heart was heavy. I hadn't spoken to Arnez since I gave him a measly ten thousand dollars to stay out of our lives. He would have taken five and the truth was that he didn't give a damn about Jacoby. I wasn't even sure if Arnez would meet him, but to settle this once and for all, I kept my word to Jacoby and called Arnez.

"Is this who I think it is?" he said, obviously having my name and number locked in his phone.

"I'm not sure who you think it is, but it's me, Kayla. How are you, Arnez? Did I catch you at a bad time?"

"Nah, not really. I'm just sitting on this bed, playing with my musty nuts and waiting for you to call me."

The thought made me want to puke. Yet again, though, I had to be careful with my words. "My call is here, but I assure you that it has nothing to do with your musty nuts. I'm calling because my son wants to see you."

He laughed then started coughing. I guessed the fool was choking because it took a minute for him to get himself together. "Excuse me. Something got caught in my throat and I had to clear it. You said *your son*, but don't you really mean *our son*?"

"My son, your son, whatever, Arnez. Jacoby wants to see you."

"How old is he now? I forgot, so tell me again."

"He's sixteen. He recently discovered that Cedric wasn't his real father and now he wants to meet you."

"Discovered, huh? Why all the fancy words when you know we don't run around here discovering shit like that everyday. We may find out that a muthafucka lied about some shit, but a discovery is kind of pushing it, don't you think?"

"I guess, but either way he found out that you are his biological father. Are you up to meeting with my son or not?"

"Just from your attitude, I can tell yo' ass is in hot water. What has Cedric done to you now? It must be something real deep because ain't no way in hell you would be calling me for anything, unless something deep is going on."

"Whatever is going on between me and Cedric is our business, not yours. Now, I'm trying to be nice, Arnez. All I want to know is if you have time to meet with Jacoby?"

"Of course I do. I tried to meet with him years ago, but you wouldn't let me, remember? You pushed me away and told me you were embarrassed—"

"All you wanted was money, so stop with the lies. You got what you wanted and that was your drugs, whores, and freedom. Don't be mad at me because things didn't work out for you."

"I see you're still the same evil bitch that you've always been. Hell, yeah, I want to see my son, but not in your presence. Take my address down and bring him to me. I'm eager to see him."

I hated that some people brought out this ugliness in me. I had a feeling that this was a bad move, but I hoped that once Jacoby got one look at this drunk, crack-smoking idiot that he would run far away from him.

"What's the address?" I asked.

Arnez gave it to me and then ended the call. I paced the floor, still not a 100-percent sure about this. Realizing that I didn't have much of a choice, I called Jacoby back to give him the address.

"I want you to go with me," he said.

"I don't want you to go at all, so please reconsider doing this. Let Arnez be, please."

"No. Now, are you going with me?"

"I don't want you to go alone, but he doesn't want me anywhere near him. We don't get along and I don't want to cause any trouble."

"I'm asking you to go with me."

I scratched my head then told Jacoby I would meet him at Adrianne's house within the hour.

When I arrived at her house, Jacoby was already outside waiting for me. I got out to give him a hug. It felt good to see my son. His hug wasn't as tight as mine, but it didn't even matter.

"I'll drive too and follow you," he said.

I nodded and not wanting to prolong this, I drove to Arnez's place that was on Martin Luther King Avenue. I parked in front of an old brick house that looked as if it would fall down if the wind blew any harder. The porch was leaning and several of the windows were cracked. Black bars covered them and the grass that was supposed to be in front of the house was mud. I knew where Arnez lived was bad, but I didn't expect for it to be *this* bad. Jacoby got out of his car first with a nervous look deep in his eyes. I tried to be the brave one, but as I got out of the car a heavyset man rolled up to me in a wheelchair. He appeared to be barely hanging on and his gray beard looked as if it hadn't been shaved in ages.

"You got any change on you, ma'am? Maybe a quarter or something."

I wasn't sure what he could buy with a quarter, but as I was about to dig in my purse, Jacoby tugged on my arm, pulling me away from the man.

"Sho' nuff," the man said. "That's how I get treated? *Daaaam*, yawl colder than a muthafucka."

We kept it moving to the front door and the man kept on rolling down the street in the wheelchair. "Bubba!" a lady yelled at him from the other side. "Butch and them lookin' for you!"

Looking for him for what? I wasn't sure. But whatever it was, Bubba got out of the wheelchair and broke out running. It was a miracle and all I could do was shake my head at the foolishness.

"I figured he was full of it," Jacoby said, then knocked on the door.

My stomach tightened and when I heard the chain being removed I could feel beads of sweat forming on my forehead. I hoped and prayed that Arnez didn't look as bad as he did when I saw him last, but when he swung the door open, his appearance was even worse. I didn't understand how a thirty-seven-year-old man could look like he was damn near sixty. He used to be one fine man, but there was no doubt that drugs, alcohol, and too many women had done him in.

"Well, well, well," Arnez said as he opened the ripped screen door. "What do we have here?"

Jacoby almost looked frightened. He stood with his eyes locked on Arnez and hadn't said a word.

"I—I know you didn't want me to come with him," I said. "But I didn't want him to come alone. May we come in?"

"Fasho," he said, and then moved aside for us to enter. As I walked past him, he inhaled and sniffed his nose close to my neck. "Damn, woman, what's that sweet perfume you wearing? Alizé?"

"Alizé is a drink and you've obviously had too many," I said, staring into his beady eyes. He seriously looked like Eddie King from *The Five Heartbeats*. I didn't know whether to laugh at his joke or cry.

Arnez laughed, though. His hazel eyes were fire red and the wavy hair he once had was all gone. He was tall like Jacoby, but much, much thinner. His lips were black and his beard was scraggly.

Jacoby looked around at the old house that badly needed renovated. It needed to be cleaned too and the smell of piss infused the air. Spiderwebs were caked in the corners and the tile floors were filthy.

"Come on in here and have a seat," Arnez said.

We followed him into a spacious living room that had a card table sitting in the middle of the floor. A sunk-in dirty couch sat in front of a window, and on the table was a glass with brown liquid in it. A joint was next to it and several cards were spread out.

"Y'all have to excuse me, but I'm getting ready for my card game with the fellas in about an hour. Anyway," he said, holding out his hand to Jacoby, "I'm Arnez. Good seeing you, man, and all I can say is you sho'll look just like me."

What an insult. Jacoby shook his hand and nodded.

"Nice to meet you," was all he said.

We sat in the aluminum chairs and Jacoby continued to look around. I wondered what he was thinking and more than anything I hoped he was grateful.

Arnez opened his arms and held them wide. "This is my palace and I'ma show y'all the rest of the crib before y'all go. Can you believe yo' mama traded all of this in for a lousy muthafucka who wasn't shit? Man, I could tell you some stories about that punk Cedric, but I want to hear about you. What you got going on, nigga?"

Jacoby shrugged his shoulders and couldn't stop gazing into his father's eyes. I knew he saw himself, even though Arnez was looking a hot mess.

"What I got going on right now is school. I already know what college I'm going to and I'm majoring in computer science, like my da—like Cedric. I play basketball, but I'm not really that good at it, and I have a girlfriend named Adrianne. We've been together for a while and I honestly think that I may one day wind up marrying her. I also play the saxophone too, but I only do that in my spare time. I want to experiment with some other instruments too, mainly the trumpet because I like how it sounds. Other than that, my life is kind of boring. I write, read, and like to bowl. I'm an A-B student and that's pretty much it about me. What about you, though? Tell me about you."

I was real proud of Jacoby. And whether my secret had caused a lot of damage or not, at that moment I realized that I may have done the right thing. A lie was still a lie, but this one I wasn't going to beat myself up about anymore.

Arnez sipped the brown liquid from the glass and cleared his throat. "Well . . . I used to have stuff like that going on, but then life happened. It can be a muthafucka, you know, and that shit can shut you down so fast that you can't even predict what's coming. Right now, I'm just chilling. I've been in rehab, trying to get my act together and I'm doing pretty good right now. Been clean for about six months, but I kick back a li'l alcohol from time to time. Other than that, I get disability because I hurt my back a while ago and I can't really do much work."

"So, like, when you were my age, what were your dreams and aspirations? I know you went to college, so what did you go for and what did you want to do? How did you know my da—Cedric, and how did you meet my mother? When did you start doing drugs and do you have any more children? How is your relationship with them and why did you accept money—"

"Whoa . . . whoa, calm down," Arnez said, then laughed. "I see you got a lot of questions for me, and I'm going to answer them for you, but I must say this to you first. I don't know what brought you to my doorstep today, but I'm glad you came. I may not ever see you again, but this moment right here is one that we will never forget. What I want to say to you is whatever disturbs your heart about me and your mother, you gotta let that shit go. I'm not shit, I ain't never gon' be shit. Even back then yo' mama knew I was fucking up. She did right by taking you from me 'cause I didn't have my head on straight. I regret that shit too, man, but there ain't a damn thing I can do about it now. If Cedric done took care of you and made you a nigga like this, I'm grateful. I mean, I gotta back the fuck up and let that man continue to handle his business, 'cause I can't. That may sound fucked up, but on a for-real tip, you are better off. I hope you know that. And now to answer all this other bullshit you done hit me with . . ."

Arnez and Jacoby went back and forth talking. I kept my mouth shut and didn't say one word. There were times when tears filled my eyes, times when I laughed with them, and times when Arnez tried his best to drag me into the conversation.

"With yo' fine self," he said, rubbing his finger along the side of my face. I smacked his hand. "Yo' mama was *soooo* good-looking back then. She fine now too, but not like she was back then. When I busted that nut, I knew I had gotten her pregnant. I sprayed that—"

"Arnez, please. You were doing just fine, and I'm sure Jacoby is not interested in details about how he was conceived."

Jacoby folded his arms across his chest and nodded. "You know, actually, I would like to hear about it."

Arnez let out a cackling laugh and pounded his fist against Jacoby's. "My nigga. You are damn sure all right with me."

They continued their conversation and as promised, Arnez gave us a tour of the rest of the house. It was awful. I felt bad for him, but he was proud of the place he called home. He talked about fixing it up and told Jacoby that if he ever needed a place to stay that he was welcome to come there. Jacoby didn't respond. Almost an hour later, we got ready to go. He and Jacoby shook hands again, hugged each other, and gave their good-byes. I watched as Jacoby walked to his car, and I turned to address Arnez before leaving.

"Thank you for that," I said. "It's what he needed and he has your number if or whenever he needs to reach you."

Arnez nodded and rubbed sweat from his head. "You did good, sugga, and I hope I didn't embarrass you too much. Jacoby got a bright future ahead of him and I can see that shit in his eyes. Now on another note: Why don't you hit me up with a few dollars? I'm broke as shit and my disability check ain't gon' get here for another week or two."

"Good-bye, Arnez. Maybe I'll call you tomorrow and take care of that for you, or maybe I won't. Whatever you do, don't hold your breath on it."

He laughed as I walked away and he watched as me and Jacoby got in our cars and drove off. I wasn't sure how Jacoby felt about today, but when we got back to Adrianne's house he came up to my car to talk.

"That was interesting," he said. "I appreciate you for calling him, but just let me chill out for a while, okay? I need time to think. Kind of get my head straight and let all of this settle in. I'm going home tonight, and just so you know, me and Cedric have been doing okay. He's been staying out of my way and I've been staying out of his. I don't know what is going on with the two of you, and I don't care to know. Work it out however you wish."

"I will."

I gave Jacoby another hug and he walked away to go into Adrianne's house. It was time for me to work out my situation with Cedric, but as soon as I got to Trina's apartment, a man was standing outside with papers in his hands.

"Kayla Thompson?"

"Yes."

He gave the papers to me and hurried to walk away. When I looked at the papers, the top read *Affidavit of Dissolution of Marriage*. My heart raced fast. I guess Cedric had finally made up his mind. I doubted that there was anything I could do to change it.

Chapter Eighteen

Trina

I was caught between a rock and a hard place. I didn't know if I should say anything or not to Kayla about what Evelyn had admitted to me, and when Kayla shared with me that Cedric had filed for a divorce, I felt terrible. I also saw it as a good thing. She could finally be rid of an asshole who meant her no good. Kayla would get the closure she needed and at this point, I felt as if there was no need for me to interfere.

I feared that if I told Kayla, she would fight for her man. She wouldn't want any woman, especially Evelyn, to have him. This thing would drag on forever and ever. Then again, maybe I was trying to justify my actions. I felt like a coward—a friend who should've known better. This was hard. Really hard, but I had to realize that I had bigger issues going on in my own life.

For the past few weeks, it had been all about Keith. We had been spending an enormous amount of time together. I had fallen head over heels for him. He was everything I needed the man in my life to be. He cooked for me, treated me with respect, lifted me up, and praised the work I'd done. He supported my endeavors and he continued to take our lovemaking sessions to new heights. I couldn't believe all of this was happening to me. It was almost frightening. I didn't know what to call myself these days: gay, straight, bisexual or what. All I knew was that I was giving my time to the one person in my life who was making me happy. Unfortunately, that person wasn't Lexi. I didn't know how to tell her when she stood outside of my apartment, begging and pleading for me to tell her where I was going, as well as who I had been spending my time with.

"Nobody," I rushed to say while walking to my car. "If there was somebody else, I would tell you."

"You never told me before." She hurried after me, damn near walking on the back of my shoes.

That pissed me off, so I spun around to face her. "All I said was that I had other friends. But I'm not in love with those friends, Lexi, nor do I have feelings for them like I have for you. So, back up. Stop tripping and go home. Please."

She rolled her eyes and tapped her foot on the ground. "Why can't I go with you? If you're not going to see anyone else, tell me why I can't go?"

I spoke through gritted teeth. "Because, I don't want you to. I need some time for myself and I'm on my way to the library. There's no need for you to be there with me, unless you're interested in reading some books. I doubt that you are, so go home and I'll call you when I'm done."

Lexi stood with tears in her eyes. I felt bad for her, but I didn't appreciate her stalking me. I turned to walk to my car, and as I got inside, she continued to stand there and mean-mug me. I drove off and went out of my way to Keith's house, just to make sure she wasn't following me. Almost forty-five minutes later, I arrived at his place.

He reached for my hand and rushed me to the third floor. "Come over here and look at this." Keith sat in a chair and stared at a painting in front of him.

I sat on his lap, observing the weird-looking painting that hadn't moved me at all. "It's . . . I guess it looks okay. I really don't like how the colors blend in together and it looks sort of sloppy to me."

Keith cocked his head back. "Sloppy? Did you just have the nerve to call my work sloppy?"

"I did, but in no way was it my intentions to hurt your feelings. It's just my honest opinion. You know I'm entitled to it, especially since you asked."

"Yes, you are entitled to it, only if I'm entitled to do this."

Keith lifted my shirt and moved my bra away from my breasts. He nibbled on my nipples and already feeling the heat, I snapped my bra loose in the back.

"Aren't you tired of all this sex we've been having?" I teased then sighed. "I know I'm getting tired of doing it, but if we must go there again, so be it."

"Yeah, unfortunately, we must."

Catching me by surprise, he dipped his brush in paint and splattered red paint on my cheek. I tried to snatch the brush from his hand, but I wound up getting more paint on me. I jumped up from his lap and as I rushed to grab a cup full of black paint, he doused me with the cup of paint in his hand. It was a good thing that white sheets were on his floor. We made one big mess, but neither of us were disappointed when the time came for us to clean up in the shower. We stood face-to-face with our wet bodies pressed against each other. Keith ran his finger along the side of my face and searched into my eyes as I gazed up at him.

"You know, there comes a time in a man's life when he knows that he has finally found that special someone in his life. For these past few weeks, I've been feeling that way. I've been feeling real good about us and it's almost like I know I found my soul mate. But then the relation-ship is so young. We're both very excited and I don't know if these feelings will fade. I'm hoping that they don't, but I wanted you to know that I can't stop thinking about you while you're away. It's driving me nuts too, because I usually can't stand to be around nobody this much. But I like you a lot, Trina. I enjoy being around you and I hope the feeling is mutual."

"Trust me when I say it is. I'm glad I found you. Things in my life are very different now."

"Wait a minute. You didn't find me. I found you."

"No, no, no, my dear. I found you. I was the one who approached you at work, remember?"

"Yes, I remember well. I walked up to you and asked if I could use your stencils. You smiled, said yes, and then I asked for your number. You must be thinking of JaQuan."

I laughed and gave Keith a kiss. "Maybe I was, but I'm not thinking about him anymore."

"Good. Now turn around and bend over so I can spank that ass for being incorrect."

I never got a spanking that felt so spectacular. Afterward, Keith cooked dinner and we chilled in his room, which was on the second floor, to watch TV. His big bed was so comfy, topped with cushiony throw pillows and a thick comforter that we cuddled in. We chomped on buttered popcorn while watching an interesting drama movie that had us tuned in. When the doorbell rang, Keith looked at the clock.

"Damn, it's a little after eleven. Who could that be?"

He tossed the comforter aside and got out of bed to go see who it was. "I'll be right back," he said. "Pause the movie for me."

As he put on his robe, I paused the movie and waited for him to come back. I wondered who was at the door. I tried to listen in to see what was up. At first, all I heard was a female's voice. Then I heard a thud and a loud gasp. I heard a door slam too and that was when I rushed out of the bed to see what was going on. From the middle staircase, I looked over the rail and could see Keith squirming around in the foyer. He was squeezing his stomach and blood covered his trembling fingers as he tried to catch his breath.

"*Keeeeeith*," I screamed and rushed down the steps. I missed a few of them and my legs buckled underneath me. I went tumbling down the stairs, but I got back up and quickly rushed up to him. He looked to be in so much pain, so I pressed my hand on top of his wound, not knowing if it was a gunshot or if he had been stabbed.

"Hold on baby," I cried out. "Please hold on! I'm going to go get you some help, okay? Hold on!"

I scurried off the floor and rushed into the living room. My bloody hands trembled as I dialed 911 and yelled into the phone for assistance.

"Help me, please! My boyfriend has been hurt! I think he's dying!"

I screamed the address into the phone then threw it down and rushed to Keith's side again. "Who did this, baby? Can you tell me who did this and why?"

Keith's eyes fluttered and shut a few times. I kept shaking him and I continued to apply pressure to his wound to stop the bleeding. I wasn't sure if what I was doing would help, but he was losing more and more blood by the minute. In a panic, I rushed up from the floor and opened the front door. I was going to get him into the car and take him to the fucking hospital myself.

"Help me!" I screamed out then turned to face him again. His eyes were closed and I released a deafening cry that echoed throughout his entire house. "*Noooooo! Please God, nooooooooo!*"

I tried to drag his body out of the front door, but he was too heavy. He opened his eyes and strained to talk to me.

"La—Lesi," he stuttered.

I wasn't sure what he was trying to say, but then it hit me. "Lexi!" I shouted. "She did this to you!"

He slowly nodded and closed his eyes again. Every single breath in me had escaped and left my body. I heard sirens coming from down the street and the blaring sounds knocked me out of my trance. I left Keith near the doorway and ran down to the middle of the street so the ambulance could see me. The paramedics moved quickly. They worked on him, he had lost so much blood. I wasn't sure if he was going to make it, but as they put him on the gurney, I squeezed his hand and kissed his cheek.

"Please don't die. Hang in there, baby, please hang in there."

The paramedics asked me to move out of the way so they could get him to the hospital that wasn't far away. I closed the front door and hurried to my car so I could follow the ambulance. They beat me there, but when I walked through the emergency room doors, I had to wait. He was in surgery. All I could do was pray for him and pray that I didn't have to go to that bitch Lexi's house and kill her.

The clock ticked away and there was still no news. At this point, no news was good news. I continued to get hit with so many questions about Keith. But pertaining to the man I cared so much about, I knew little about him. I mean, I couldn't answer much. All I knew was his first and last name, where he worked, what he did for a living, his birthday, and his address. I didn't know how to contact his parents, nor did I know how to reach out to his brother, who he was really close with. I had no idea who his insurance carrier was, or even if he *had* insurance. His phone was back at his house, as well as his wallet. I was sure those things would be helpful to me, but before I left the hospital, I asked the nurse if she could give me some kind of update on his condition.

"Please tell me something. Anything that you know right now would be helpful," I begged.

The nurse told me to wait, where I stood for a few minutes. She came back almost ten minutes later and touched my hand. "The doctors are still working on him. You have to believe that they're doing the best they can. Just say a little prayer and everything will be all right. As soon as I know something, I'll let you know."

I wiped my flowing tears and nodded. Wanting to go get Keith's information and call his family, I got in my car. I felt so horrible because this was all my fault. I should have told Lexi about my feelings for him. I knew how possessive she was and it was my fault that things had escalated like this. I reached for my cell phone in my purse and called Kayla. She answered my phone and I was so glad she was at my place.

"Kayla, Lexi stabbed Keith. I'm at the hospital. I really need somebody right—"

"Oh my God!" she shouted. "Is he okay? Where are you?"

"I don't know if he's going to make it, but I'm at Barnes-Jewish Hospital on Kings highway."

"I'm on my way."

Kayla hung up. I thought about calling Evelyn, but unfortunately, she just wasn't that kind of friend. She was trouble and right now I didn't need trouble. I put my phone back into my purse, and as soon as I started my car, I felt a sharp blade touching the side of my neck. I was getting ready to turn around, but Lexi told me not to bother.

"How dare you cry over a dumb-ass nigga like this? What happened to us, Trina! Huh! Is this how you want to play me!"

My whole body was stiff. I didn't dare move. I did, however, look in the rearview mirror at her. She appeared very unstable.

"Pu—put the knife down, Lexi. You don't want to do this and you've already done enough."

"Is that muthafucka dead? That's when I'll know if I've done enough!"

I had to think fast and do my best to calm her. I was nervous as ever and could feel sweat sliding down the side of my face.

"Yes, he is dead. I didn't want to tell Kayla that he was, but you killed him. It's all over with and you don't have to worry about him anymore. It's you and me, again; forever and just like it was before."

I could hear Lexi breathing heavy. Never in my wildest dreams did I expect for anything like this to happen. How was I to know that I had been sleeping with a crazy bitch like her? She was way off.

My eyes shifted as I looked around for a police officer, security guard or somebody to help me. Unfortunately for me, though, there weren't too many people close by us.

Lexi pressed the knife harder and I felt a sting. I could feel blood trickle down my neck and I had no idea how deep she had cut me. I did know, however, that I needed to do something fast.

"It can never be like it was before," she cried out. "You played me, Trina! I loved you with all of my heart and you *plaaaaayed* me!"

"I'm sorry, but please know that I loved you too. I still love you and I promise you we can work this out. But if you do something stupid, we can't. We can't be together if you do something stupid and I know you don't want that."

Right then, I saw a police officer pull his car near the emergency room entrance and get out. I lifted my hand, slamming it against the horn. It sounded off so loudly that Lexi jumped halfway over the seat and began swinging the knife around. She stabbed everywhere she could, missing my face and head by inches. I hurried to loosen my seat belt and tried to unlock the door with her all over me. The knife cut deep into my shoulder and when I fell out of the car, I yelled out for help. The policeman was already headed in my direction and before Lexi got out of the car, he pulled out his gun and aimed it at her.

"Put the knife down or I'll shoot," he yelled.

Lexi was too anxious to get at me. She ignored the cop's warning and in a rage, jumped out of the car to get at me as I lay on the ground. Once she raised the knife in the air, the officer fired one shot that whistled right into her chest, blowing it wide open. As her limp body fell on top of me, I covered my mouth with my hands and screamed out as loud as I could.

Chapter Nineteen

Evelyn

After meeting with Trina, I was kind of hoping my phone would ring or that Kayla would come knocking on my door to confront me. I prepared myself on what to say to her. It was along the lines of exactly what I'd said to Trina. Unfortunately, I hadn't had the opportunity to spill my guts yet. Kayla hadn't called, but Trina called about an hour ago, telling me she was at the hospital with her boyfriend Keith. She said he had been stabbed and that she had been injured as well. She didn't sound good at all. It seemed as if there was more to the story that she wasn't telling me. So trying to be nosy and to give her some support, I put on my summer dress and headed out.

The moment I walked out the door, the wind picked up and blew up my dress. It was kind of flimsy and I hoped nobody got a peek at my turquoise thong. After I left the hospital, I planned to stop by Cedric's house to see him. He'd been working from home lately and he said Jacoby wasn't always there. That was a good thing, because we did need some privacy.

I arrived at the hospital around nine o'clock that morning. I wasn't sure where Trina was, so I called her on my cell phone to see what was up. She directed me to go to the waiting room and said she would be there shortly. When I got there, I saw Kayla sitting in one of the chairs, paging through a magazine. I eased over to her because

I didn't know yet if Trina had said anything to her. I wasn't sure if she would come out swinging on me, so I paid attention to her expression. She lifted her head and smiled when she saw me coming her way. She then stood up and when I approached her, she gave me a hug.

"It's about time you got here," she said.

I sighed, knowing that everything was good; at least for now, anyway. "Trina just called me this morning. What happened and how long have you been here?"

Kayla gave me the scoop about what had happened, but I was still a little confused.

"So, this backstabbing, no-good fool had a girlfriend? If that's the case, then he deserved what he got. A scorned woman is nothing to play with, and some men need to stop trying to date all these women at one time. I don't understand why Trina is sticking by him. If it were me, I would be out of here."

"That's not what happened. I'll let Trina give you the details of what happened. But I can assure you that you're barking up the wrong tree."

"I don't see how. We see this kind of stuff happening all the time. Man cheats, woman gets mad and kills him."

Kayla caught an attitude with me. "Again," she snapped. "That's not what happened. If you want to know the truth about something, I'll share this. Keith is really a good guy. He didn't deserve this and that's all I'm going to say."

"Well, I'm not sure if you know the meaning of a good guy. You think Cedric is a good guy, but we both know that he isn't."

Kayla cocked her head back and frowned. "Are you okay this morning? You're coming off real strong and your attitude is horrible."

"I'm fine. Maybe being pregnant has me on edge a little. You know how that goes."

Kayla smiled and lightly smacked her forehead. "Oh, forgive me. With all that's been going on, do you know that I forgot you were pregnant? We haven't spoken much lately, and I want you to know that you're always in my thoughts and prayers, no matter what."

This heifer was so fake. Now, how do you forget that your best friend is pregnant? That made no sense to me and this was an example of the problem I had with Kayla. If it didn't revolve around her, she wasn't interested.

As we were sitting in the waiting area, in walked a dark-skinned, attractive man with locks. I paused my conversation with her to take a look. He walked up to the snack machine and then to the soda machine. When he came over to us, I gazed up at his sexy self.

"Here," he said, handing Kayla a soda. "I figured you may want something to drink."

"Thank you," she said, and then turned to me. "Bryson, this is Evelyn. She's my and Trina's best friend. Evelyn, this is Bryson, Keith's brother."

"Nice to meet you," I said with a smile. He shook my hand and said the pleasure was all his.

Bryson gave us the scoop on Keith's condition. From what he said, Keith pulled through surgery and was now in serious, but stable, condition. His parents were with him. So was Trina.

He looked at Kayla. "She told me to tell you to go home, get some rest, and said she would call you later."

"Well, you tell her that I'm staying right here. I want to make sure she's okay. I'm not leaving until I know for sure."

Bryson smiled and walked away. If Trina wanted us to leave, I really didn't want to stay. But I did so anyway, just so she could see me there during her time of need. There was no telling when I would need her to be there for me. It did bother me, though, that Kayla had always seemed to be there more for Trina than she was for me. It had been this way for a long time, so I added that to my list of gripes about her.

About fifteen minutes later, Trina came into the waiting room looking worn-out. Her sweats were hanging low. Her tennis shoes were untied and she had on an oversized T-shirt that was too big. I couldn't believe she was up here representing herself like this in front of Keith's parents. I figured they weren't impressed by their son's choices in women. I cut her some slack, considering the situation, but still.

She came up to me and Kayla with a somber look on her face. The first thing she did was thank me for coming and then she sat in a chair across from us and crossed her legs. She started to tie her tennis shoes and then slowly shook her head.

"I can't believe all of this is happening," she said. "Keith is doing better, but he's not out of the woods yet. He lost a lot of blood and she stabbed him like three times in his stomach. I don't know how he made it through this. The more I think about it, I can't help but to think about how all of this is my fault."

Trina covered her face and started to cry. Kayla rushed over to the seat next to her and hugged her. "No, it's not your fault. I know Keith does not believe that, either. Some people just do crazy things sometimes and this matter was beyond your control."

I sat there clueless. Now, why in the heck would Trina think this was all her fault? It was Keith's fault for being a player. Was she actually sitting there taking responsibility for him? I swear, I had some stupid-ass girlfriends. They needed to get their acts together. Maybe I was missing something, but this was ridiculous. Either way, I played along with it and offered my support too by going to sit next to her.

"I don't know why you see this as your fault, but it's not," I said, rubbing her back. "Calm down. You have to believe that Keith will make a full recovery."

Trina seemed to lean more toward Kayla, so I backed away. They looked at each other, and then Trina turned to me.

"Can we go somewhere and talk?" she asked.

I assumed she wanted to talk to me about my situation with Cedric, but I wasn't up to hearing it right now. "Later," I said. "We'll talk later, especially since I think I already know what it's about."

Trina stood up. "No, you don't know. Let's go somewhere and talk now."

She seemed adamant, so I stood up and followed her. We walked together to the cafeteria, where Trina sat at a table that was far away from others.

"Listen," I said, taking a seat in the chair across from her. "This is the wrong time to be bringing up my relationship with Cedric. If you're worried about me saying anything to Kayla, I won't. I told you I'm not going to tell her, but I'm shocked that you haven't said anything."

"I'm not going to tell her. I truly believe that you should be the one to come clean. But I didn't bring you here to talk about that. I wanted to tell you about a secret I've kept for a long time and through keeping that secret is why I'm here today. Maybe me telling you this will make you spill the truth. And believe me when I say it's a very bad feeling when you know you're responsible for hurting the people you care about."

I shrugged. "Yeah, well, some of those people have hurt me too. But what's your secret?"

Trina swallowed the huge lump I saw forming in her throat. "Evelyn, I've been involved—meaning intimately involved—in relationships with women for the past several years. When my relationship with BJ ended, I made the decision not to ever date another man, because he had done me so wrong. I started seeing that chick, Lexi, and our relationship got real serious. I kept that relationship a secret and then I met Keith. To make a long story short and without getting into more details, Lexi was the one who stabbed Keith. She was shot dead on the parking lot outside yesterday, and the police shot her in her attempt to kill me."

I hadn't moved, hadn't blinked . . . nothing. Did she just tell me she was a dyke? This had to be a joke. I assumed that Trina had fabricated this story, making it so tragic that I would be convinced to tell Kayla the truth.

"That was pretty good, Trina, and it was also pretty low. I'm not going to tell Kayla what is going on, and if you think your little story about Lexi and Keith is going to move me then you're sadly mistaken. And the whole gay thing is ridiculous. You love dick too much to go that route and I know that for a fact."

"Do you? Really? I guess you may need to open your eyes and reflect on the last several years, then. You haven't seen me with many men, and if you have, there's been no connection between us. I hadn't talked about them and besides all of that, I would never, ever lie to you about something like this. As my friend, I wanted you to know the truth. I've been holding onto this for so long, and now other people's lives have been affected."

I was trying to read Trina. What I discovered from the look in her eyes was that she was telling the truth. All kinds of crazy thoughts swam in my head, and I kept thinking about the many times I got undressed in front of her, how many times I hugged her, and the many times she put her lips on my cheeks. I couldn't do this shit, and no best friend of mine could be this way and not tell me.

"So, let me get this straight," I said as more anger crept on my face. "You're a lesbian, but you're in love with Keith. Your girlfriend tried to kill him and then she tried to kill you. After twenty-plus years of friendship, you're coming clean today because you feel guilty for destroying other people's lives. Does that about sum up everything you've told me?"

Trina stared at me from across the table. "I knew you wouldn't get it, Evelyn. You just don't have it in you to understand—"

"Understand," I said, raising my voice. "No, I do understand, Trina, and I understand things very well. I bet any amount of money that Kayla knows about this and has known for some time. The two of you have never been real friends to me, and I'm always the one being left out and dismissed like I'm not shit! This whole BFF stuff is a bunch of bullshit and it has been so for a very long time. If friends come in the form of you and Kayla, guess what? *I . . . don't . . . want . . . no . . . friends!* To hell with you both and you can take your pussy-eating-ass back in there and tell Kayla what I said. The next thing you're going to be telling me is the two of you are fucking each other and you want to hook up for a threesome. That wouldn't surprise me one bit and the two of you deserve each other."

I stood and tucked my purse underneath my arm. "Give Keith my condolences. I hope that whenever he comes out of this, he realizes the kind of woman you really are and he runs like hell to get away from you."

I stormed off. Many people's heads were turned in my direction and whispers filled the room, but I didn't care. I got the hell out of there and called Cedric to see if he was home. He didn't answer, but I still drove to his house anyway.

I parked in the curvy driveway, right behind a car that I hadn't seen before. I assumed that the car belonged to one of Cedric's business partners, but when I got to the glass doors that viewed into the house, I could see Cedric sitting on the couch in the great room. His head was dropped back and his eyes were closed. I thought he was sleeping, but as soon as I lifted my hand to ring the doorbell, I saw the long, black hair of a woman whose head was in his lap. It was apparent that her mouth was going to be burning too, and Cedric simply could not get enough. I was already in a bad mood, but he would never see me act a fool and go crazy about him being with other women. It did sting a little, especially after he seemed so decent the other night and had come off like he was getting serious about us.

Instead of ringing the doorbell, I stood for a few minutes, watching the action. Cedric looked to be faking it and the woman kept looking up at him for approval. She appeared to be real young and she was probably the one who had given him chlamydia. I wondered if he was giving her money like he was me, and thinking about her cutting into his cash was what prompted me to ring the doorbell. Cedric snapped his head to the side and a few minutes later he tied his robe and came to open the door.

"I see that you're busy, but do you mind if I come in?" I asked.

"It would be nice for you to call. That way you don't interrupt me. What is it that you want this time, Evelyn?"

"For starters, did you know that bitch Trina was gay?"

I had to say something that would get his attention. He laughed and that was when I took the opportunity to ease inside. "I promise to be good and I have nothing to say to your midday trick," I said. "I'm going to your office, so meet me there as soon as you can."

Cedric shook his head as I walked away. I passed through the great room, eyeing the young chick as she stood and wiped her mouth.

"Do—"

"Evelyn, don't," Cedric warned. "Go to my office. I'll be there shortly."

I kept my mouth shut. Didn't want to say anything to the stupid broad who probably had no clue what she was getting herself into, like Kayla. I knew Cedric more than anybody did. He had taught me a lot, even within the last month. The truth was, Cedric didn't give a damn about anybody. His love was for the almighty dollar and that was it. Women were good for one thing and one thing only. That was sex. Love didn't live in his heart anymore and thanks to Kayla's lies it hadn't lived there in a long time.

See, he and I had a lot in common. That was why Cedric appreciated me, more than he did anyone. I wasn't the kind of woman who griped all the time about every little thing, but if I ever felt that he had crossed the line he would surely hear about it. The chlamydia thing crossed the line. And the way he spoke to me that day made me look at him in a different way. He showed his true colors. I had to prepare myself better for what was to come.

I sat on a comfy sofa in Cedric's office with my legs crossed. The bay window brought in much light, but some of the light was blocked by the silky brown curtains that draped down to the floor. His oak-wood desk was cluttered with papers and the bookshelf behind his desk was filled with books. Cedric was a brilliant man and even though he had his flaws, I admired a man who knew how to make millions. For that I gave him credit. Relationship-wise he wasn't shit. I saw a picture of him and Jacoby on his desk, but there were no pictures whatsoever of him and Kayla. Not even on the twenty-seven-inch monitor that sat on his desk or on the walls, where there were pictures of him and his business partners.

The door squeaked open and he came inside. A cigar dangled from the corner of his mouth and he tightened his robe before taking a seat behind his desk.

"You know I got work to do, so shoot. What's up?"

"Did you know Trina was a lesbian?"

"Yes. I've known for a long time. I'm surprised that it seems to be breaking news for you. I told Kayla that I thought she was, but she didn't believe me."

"So, Kayla didn't know?"

"She may know now, but as of a month ago she told me I was out of my mind for telling her something like that."

"Well, Trina told me about her status today. Her boyfriend was shot by her lover, and the police killed her lover for trying to kill her."

"What? I didn't know she had a boyfriend."

"It's that Keith dude. Anyway, enough about them. What's up with you and Miss Youngin'? Is she the one who gave us chlamydia?"

"Don't start that shit again, all right? Did you take your pills?"

"Of course I did and I can tell you this right now. We won't have sex again without using condoms. I mean it, Cedric, and when you come to me you need to be prepared. I know I will."

"Just like you were prepared the other night, right? Let that bullshit go, Evelyn, you're better than that and no need to be petty."

"It's not being petty. You should be more careful, especially since you enjoy sex so much. You're too old for me to be schooling you, so I'm going to move on to the next subject. That would be my living arrangements. Without me working, I can't keep up with the rent. I'm not sure if I'll be able to find a job soon or not, and with me being pregnant I don't know if I can handle work anyway. So, I've been thinking. You have plenty of room here, and as you can see from my reaction to your head blower, I won't get in the way. When the baby is born, I'll already have everything set up. I'll cook, keep the house clean for you, and I'll continue to make myself available to you sexually. Now, what man would want more than that?"

Cedric responded by shaking his head. "Sometimes, I wonder about you, Evelyn. There are times when I wholeheartedly admire you, and then there are times when I honestly believe you need to see a shrink. I see that you've put much thought into this, but let me stop you before you get ahead of yourself. Jacoby is my son, and in case you forgot, he lives here too. I get that you're pregnant, but since our last conversation I've given this situation more thought. I don't think it's a good idea for us to live together, or be together as a couple, because I have too many things going on that you won't approve of. I may decide to make arrangements for you and the baby to live in a better place that is suitable for the two of you. The loft that you have isn't bad, and if rent money is what you need, I'll see what I can do. Meanwhile, you do need to get back to work, because I will not be supporting you. As far as the pussy thing goes, you're not doing me any favors by making yourself available to me. So are many other women, so your pussy ain't a big deal."

Cedric occasionally irritated me by saying the wrong things. I stood and walked over to his desk. "It sounds like you're trying to leave me out in the cold, but I told myself that I wouldn't come here to argue with you, so I won't. But let's be clear about some things then we can figure out the correct way to move forward. Jacoby is not your son and you know it. You've been playing the fatherly role for too long to a child that isn't yours. It's time to give it up." I pointed to my stomach. "This baby here, however, is yours. He or she will be your first. He or she will carry on your legacy, so therefore, he or she will need to be your number-one priority. With that, all I'm asking is that you consider what I said. I thought it was a wonderful offer, but please know that the offer won't stay on the table for too long. Let me know what's up soon. As for now, I'm going to let you get back to what you call work."

"Thank you. Be sure to close the door behind you and try like hell to have a good day."

"Oh, you too."

I rolled my eyes at him and walked out, thinking that his ass may have been better off dead than he was alive.

Chapter Twenty

Kayla

So much had been happening that I hadn't made much time for myself. I was doing my best to be there for Trina, and being there for her helped push to the back of my mind all that was going on with my life. Trina told me about her conversation with Evelyn and the way she reacted was a shame. Then I thought about my reaction too and understood how Evelyn probably felt betrayed. Still, I left it up to them to settle their differences. When all was said and done I was sure they would.

The one thing I was glad about was that I had been speaking to Jacoby more. He'd been calling me and I'd been calling to check up on him. Everything seemed to be okay with him, but he did tell me that he thought a new relationship with Arnez wasn't the right thing to pursue now. I was glad that he had made that decision and it was a decision that only he could make. It took him to see Arnez in that condition for Jacoby to realize he wanted no part of it.

We talked about Cedric filing for divorce and Jacoby asked what I intended to do. Right then, I wasn't sure. I was on my way to see a lawyer, just so I could know what my options were. Unfortunately, I had signed a prenup back in the day, saying that if we ever divorced, what belonged to him was his and what belonged to me was mine. I signed that stupid thing, having no idea that Cedric would one day make all of this money. Surely we both had hopes that things would prosper, but I never envisioned that it would get to this level. Apparently, he did. He was always ten steps ahead of me and I regretted that he was in control of so many things, including my life.

Before meeting with the lawyer, I stopped by Cedric's office to see if he was there. I was banned from entering the building, but the receptionist told me that Cedric was working from home. Knowing that Jacoby was at school, I drove to the house so I could look him face-to-face and be sure that this divorce was what he really wanted. When I got there, however, I saw Evelyn's car parked in the driveway. I had no idea what she was doing there and the fact that she was kind of upset me. I drove past the house, but as I turned around at the end of the street, that was when I saw her coming out the front door. A mean mug was on her face and she shielded her eyes with glasses. She hopped into her car and sped off down the street, going real fast.

After she left, I pulled in the driveway. I went to the door and it was unlocked. I walked inside and looked around. I missed being here and this still felt like home to me. I heard Cedric talking to someone and made my way back to his office, where he was. When I opened the door, his conversation came to a halt.

"Clay, let me call you back," he said through speakerphone. "Give me a minute to look that up, okay?"

"Sure. Call me back when you check that out for me."

Cedric clicked the button to end the call.

"I just ran into Evelyn—well, not really ran into her, but she sped off before I pulled up. What was she doing here?"

"What do you think she was doing here?"

"I don't know. That's why I asked."

"Money, Kay. She came here to ask me for some money. I told her to get the hell out of here and she left upset. I guess since she hasn't been able to hit you up for cash anymore, she thought she could come over here and ask me. It's not going down like that and you know it."

I couldn't believe that Evelyn was that darn desper-
ate—then again, yes, I could. She knew better, didn't she,
and what nerve? I made a mental note to call her and go
off on her for doing something so sneaky and ridiculous.

"Well, I'm glad you didn't give her one dime. I'll be sure
to call and talk to her about her greed later."

"Don't worry about it. You know that people try to hit
me up all the time for money and you've had experience
with that too. I don't want her to feel embarrassed, so just
let it go."

Cedric was right. Besides, I wasn't there to talk about
Evelyn. I was there to talk about us. "I will let it go, but I
don't want to let our marriage go. I received the divorce
papers the other day and I can't tell you how much my
heart is bleeding right now. I think this can be worked
out, Cedric. I also think you're making a big mistake. I
haven't been perfect, I've made plenty of mistakes, but
so have you. Can't you forgive me, as I've forgiven you?
I've been so miserable and I'm here to claim my life back
again. I want to come home and be the best wife that I can
be to you, and the best mother that I can be to Jacoby.
Allow me to do that and let's end all of this nonsense
today."

Cedric put his hands behind his head and swayed back
and forth in his leather swivel chair. "I wish it were that
easy, Kay, but it's not. I am not trying to hurt you by
divorcing you and you need to be clear about one thing:
Love. I don't love you anymore. I have not loved you for a
very long time. I have no other choice but to set you free
and get on with my life. I'm not going to make this hard
for you and it's not like I'm going to leave you out there in
the streets. I just don't want you here, living in this house
with me anymore. My advice is that you consult with
your attorney, have him check out what I proposed, and
let's get this rolling as amicably and quickly as possible.
Delaying this process will be the only thing that hurts.

Don't continue to do that to yourself and one day you'll realize this divorce is for the best."

I stood in front of Cedric with tears streaming down my face. It had finally hit me that this was the end of us, of our family, of everything I had always wanted. I had given up so much for him, as well as for my son. This pain I wouldn't wish on my worst enemy and to hear Cedric say that he didn't love me anymore tore at my heart and soul.

"Please," I begged as tears rolled over my trembling lips. My hands were shaking and I felt as if I were on the brink of a nervous breakdown. My heart was heavy and I could hear it pounding rapidly against my chest. "Don't do this to me. This is not about you giving me money and please know that money will not heal my broken heart. I still love you, Cedric, and you're just still bitter about me lying to you. That anger will pass and . . . and you will—"

"No. No, I won't forgive you and I will never forgive you. I know how hard this is for you, and if you need counseling I'll be happy to pay for it. But this is done, baby. This marriage is done and you will have to accept that."

I could barely catch my breath from crying so hard. Cedric was so cold. I couldn't bear to stand there and allow him to see me so broken like this. I wiped my flowing, salty tears and turned to face the door.

"I am sorry that it has to be this way, Kay, but you brought this on yourself."

I didn't bother to respond. Maybe I did bring this on myself and now my chickens had come home to roost. I staggered my way to the door like a zombie. When I got to the car, I dropped my head on the steering wheel and clenched my chest. "This isn't over," I said in a whisper. "By no means is this over with yet."

While sitting in my car thinking, I called Evelyn to see why she had stopped by to see Cedric. She didn't answer, but I left a voice mail, telling her to meet me at Trina's place. It was time to get to the bottom of this.

Chapter Twenty-one

Cedric

I was a man who, with no question, had a conscience. Seeing Kayla that way broke my heart, but the damage was already done. With all that had been going on with me and Evelyn, there was no turning back. With all the lies that Kayla had told, there was no way for me to ever forgive her. I couldn't go back to the life we once shared and things weren't always like this. But today was a new day. I wanted my freedom and I wanted her to go seek the happiness she deserved.

Thinking about all that had been transpiring, I massaged my forehead and lowered my head on the edge of my desk, lightly pounding it to knock out my headache. I wanted to go get some aspirin, but my body and eyes were so tired from not getting much sleep these days that I found myself fading. Resting my eyes caused me to enter into a deep sleep, but I woke up about an hour or so later.

My headache was still throbbing, so I got up to go to the kitchen. As I passed by the stairs, I heard the floor squeak from upstairs and thought it was Jacoby.

"Jacoby, is that you?" I yelled up the stairs. There was no answer and when I looked at the clock on the wall it was after six o'clock, so I figured he was home.

I jogged up the stairs and entered his bedroom. He wasn't there, so I turned off his TV that must have been on all day. I roamed his room being nosy, and when

I picked up a picture that sat near his computer of us playing basketball, I smiled. Jacoby was a good kid and my son or not, I still intended to look out for him. I hated that he was caught in the middle of all of this, but I wanted him to know the truth about me not being his real father. I could have told him a while back, but in my world timing was everything.

I heard footsteps again, so I put the picture down and proceeded down the hallway to my bedroom. One door was already opened, but when I opened the other one, I was met with the barrel of a shotgun that was aimed directly at my face. The person holding it was in disguise. All I could see at first were the eyes behind the black mask that was pulled over the person's head. I tried to quickly decipher if the body behind the baggy clothes was that of a man or woman, but I couldn't.

"Wha—what do you want?" I asked in fear, with my hands in the air. "Take anything you—"

No response, so I continued to plead with my intruder. "Please," I begged. "Don't do this. I'll give you anything you want. What is it that you want?"

The intruder released one hand from the trigger and placed one finger against her lips, as a gesture for me to be quiet. The lips looked kind of familiar to me, but I still couldn't make them out. As she took several steps forward, I backed up. When she moved, I moved. I paid close attention to the sway of her hips, trying to get myself familiar with who they belonged to. I wasn't there yet, but I was getting there.

I stopped backing up at the top of the stairs and as the shotgun remained aimed at my face, it hit me. I knew who was behind the mask, but the moment I opened my mouth, she lowered the gun and squeezed the trigger. All I remembered was the loud, blasting sound that popped my eardrum. I saw fire spark from the gun and I felt myself tumbling down the carpeted stairs. The ceiling was spinning and my entire body was numb. My eyes watered, but I could see a blurred vision of the woman standing over me. She pulled the mask over her head and wiggled her fingers through her hair.

"Don't you know, Cedric," she said with a smile on her face. "Too much pussy ain't good for you."

After that, my eyes fluttered some more, and I saw darkness with a flash of white, bright lights.

Chapter Twenty-two

Trina

Thank God Keith was doing much better, but he would have to stay in the hospital for some days yet. I spent every hour that I could by his side, making sure that he would be okay. I was also very appreciative of Kayla being by my side, but as for Evelyn, she had seriously let me down. I don't know why I expected anything different from her. I should have prepared myself better for her reaction. I didn't know if we would ever be able to mend our friendship again, but I was at a point where I didn't care anymore.

Keith turned in bed and looked at me sitting in a chair with my legs pressed against my chest. The room was kind of chilly, but I did have a blanket over me to stay warm. Keith had beads of sweat on his forehead. He cocked his head from side to side while looking at me.

"You're still here," he said with a slight smile.

"Where else am I going?"

"I don't know. You could go to work, go for a walk, to the mall . . . something."

"Nope. I'd rather be here with you—that's if you don't mind."

"Of course not."

He licked his dry lips and looked around at the get-well-soon balloons and many cards. They were from coworkers, family, and friends. Keith had a lot of love, as well as support.

"Have my mother and father been here?"

"They were here earlier, but you were sleeping. Your mother said she would be back around seven and your dad said he was coming back tomorrow."

"That's cool."

Keith looked around the room again and then he stared out the window for a minute.

"Can I get you anything?" I asked.

"Nah, I'm just thinking. I never came that close to death and it's a scary feeling. I'm just grateful to be alive and see all of this around me."

I stood up and walked up to the bed. I took his hand, squeezing it with mine. "I'm grateful too and I wanted to tell you how sorry I am for putting you in the middle of my relationship with Lexi. I had no idea that she was crazy like that and you have no idea how horrible I feel for my mistakes."

"It's not your fault. I wouldn't necessarily say that Lexi was crazy. It's just that love can make you do some crazy things sometimes. I don't know if you told her about us or not, but maybe you should have. Then again, it may not have made a difference, because I'm sure that losing a woman like you wouldn't be easy for anyone."

"I'm glad you can see it like that, but to me she was crazy."

I told him about Lexi being shot and killed by the police. I also showed him the numerous stitches I'd gotten from where she stabbed me. He couldn't believe it. He chuckled and retracted on his statement.

"Maybe she was a bit coo-coo then, but all I'm saying is if the mind isn't as strong as the broken heart is, you'll have a problem. My suggestion: Always be honest with people. The truth may hurt, but it'll set you free every time."

Keith was so right. We talked for a while longer and I couldn't help but to think about the secret I was keeping from Kayla. Whether the truth about Cedric and Evelyn would hurt her or not, she needed to know. I wanted to set myself free and get all of what I had known about Evelyn's and Cedric's relationship off my chest. I didn't want a repeat of what had happened to Keith and this time there would be no blood on my hands. With that in mind, I stayed with him for a little while longer. I then prepared myself to go home and tell Kayla the truth.

I bent over Keith's bed, giving him a lengthy kiss. "I'm getting ready to go home and take care of a few things. I'll be back tomorrow, okay?"

"That's fine, but when you come back tomorrow will you do me a favor and bring me something real sweet?"

"*Daaang*, you got me. What more do you want?"

He chucked a little and held his stomach. "I didn't know I had all of you, but that's good to know."

"All of me and then some. And that's just a little something that I thought you should know. Now, as for the sweet thing you're in need of, tell me what you want and I'll bring it to you."

"Are you good at baking cakes?"

"It depends on what kind of cake you want. Duncan Hines, Betty Crocker . . . what?"

"Homemade. One of those homemade, buttery pound cakes with that light glaze on top. My grandmother used to bake those all the time. I would love to have one of those."

"I know exactly what you're talking about, but you told me to be honest with you, so I will. I can't go there like that and any cake that I make you will not be homemade. I will do my best to make you one very close to it, and are you sure you're supposed to be eating that kind of stuff already?"

"I would love to be eating you, but I'm settling right now, all right? Do your best on the cake and I'll appreciate whatever you bring me tomorrow, even if it's a Snickers bar."

I laughed and leaned in to give him another kiss before leaving. On my way home, I stopped at the grocery store to see what I could put together. I wanted to bake the cake from scratch, but I didn't have a good recipe. I did have my cell phone, though, so I looked up the ingredients on the Internet and filled my cart with the items I needed. I also got Duncan Hines cake mix, just in case the home-made cake didn't pan out for me.

As I waited in line to pay for my groceries, I spotted Cynthia waiting in another line. She was with another lady I recognized from church, but I didn't know her name. They appeared to be real chummy with each other. I turned my head to ignore them. What Cynthia had going on wasn't my business anymore, and it was so funny that I now found myself not attracted to her.

The clerk rang up my groceries and when the bagger put them into my cart I strolled out the door. I put the bags in my trunk, but as soon as I opened my car door, Cynthia came up to me.

"You're not going to speak," she said.

"Oh, hey, Cynthia. I'm sorry. I didn't see you."

"Yes you did. I saw you watching me in there, and don't be jealous because you were the one who started acting funny with me. You didn't expect for me to wait around for you to get your act together, did you?"

"No, I really didn't. And if you're happy, I'm happy. Just do yourself a favor and come clean with Pastor Clemons. I know the hurt behind what he has done to you is making you this way, but tell him how you're feeling inside and go to counseling. Maybe the two of you can work things out, maybe y'all can't. But what you're doing to yourself is no good. In the end. Somebody may wind up getting hurt."

Cynthia threw her hand back at me. "I hear enough preaching on Sundays. Thanks for the advice, but save it for someone who needs it. My husband and I will be just fine. I do appreciate your concern for him, especially since you're in love with his wife. Unfortunately, sweetheart, I'm taken."

She walked away, sashaying her hips from side to side. The other lady was eyeing me, trying to see what was up. She wasn't going to catch any hell from me. I was done; finished with that mess, and the only love on my mind right now was Keith.

I entered my apartment, wondering if Kayla would be there. She wasn't, but I was surprised to see Evelyn standing outside of my door.

"What are you doing here?" I asked in a snobby tone.

"I got a call from Kayla. She wanted me to meet her here so we could talk. I need to get some things off my chest too, so I thought it would be wise to stop by and chat with the both of you."

Without saying a word, I put the key in the door to unlock it. Evelyn took a seat on the couch while I put up the groceries and went to change into my jeans and a T-shirt. While in my bedroom, I kept rehearsing in my head how I was going to break the news to Kayla about Evelyn and Cedric. Then again, maybe Evelyn was here to do it. She said that she wanted to get some things off her chest, but that could mean anything. I pondered about what I could say to get this mess out in the open, just in case Evelyn wouldn't step up to the plate.

"They've been having sex . . . screwing each other . . . no, fucking," I mumbled. "He doesn't love her and I think. . . . no, I want you to stay strong, and screw him. Let them stay together . . . girl, fight for your marriage and to hell with Evelyn."

I didn't know how to break it down to Kayla, so I let out a deep sigh and returned to the living room where Evelyn was. Before I could say one word, Kayla came through the door. Her braids were gone and almost all of her hair had been cut off. I was surprised to see her hair shorter than mine, but the nearly bald cut looked decent on her. It showed the roundness of her face more and it also revealed her almond-shaped, pretty eyes. Her eyes showed sadness, though, and I could see the puffiness underneath them. It was obvious that today wasn't a good day. I assumed that she had just finished meeting with her attorney. Evelyn stood to look at Kayla, but she didn't say a word.

"So how did it go?" I asked, referring to her meeting.

Kayla appeared to be out of it. She walked slowly into the living room and sat on the couch. "How did what go?"

"The meeting with your attorney. What did he say?"

"I didn't go. I changed my mind about meeting with him."

My brows rose as I sat in the chair next to her. Evelyn sat back down too and started to question Kayla. "Why? What changed your mind?"

Kayla moved her head from side to side. "I . . . I just don't want a divorce. I'm not giving up and I'm going to fight to save my family."

"But you can't save your family, Kayla," I said. "What's done is done. Don't you think you should consider moving on?"

"I am moving on. I'm moving out of here by the end of the week and I'm going back home. I'm going home to be with my husband and son."

"I don't think so," Evelyn said. "That wouldn't be a good idea."

"Why not?" Kayla hissed. "And why are you always being so negative?"

Evelyn folded her arms across her chest. "I'm not always being negative, but the question is, Why did you ask me to come here?"

Kayla squeezed her forehead and frowned. "Forget it, Evelyn. I was thinking crazy stuff when I called and told you to meet me here. The truth is, how I feel about you right now doesn't really matter."

"Well, it matters to me. And now that we're all here, I have a few things that I want to say." She looked at me first. "I apologize for how I treated you at the hospital, but please understand that your news was very hard for me to swallow. I thought about it over and over again. And you know what, Trina? Do you. Who am I to judge you, when I have my skeletons too?"

She was right about that, but I wasn't worried about my friendship with Evelyn. There was a bigger issue and it revolved around her and Kayla. I figured the day would come when we would reconcile our differences, yet I was surprised that Evelyn had approached me first. Normally, I would be the one who reached out to her.

"Your apology is accepted and I apologize for saying some of the hurtful things that I said to you too. But we all need to stop with the lies. If we're going to call ourselves friends, then we need to start acting like real friends, instead of haters. Is there anything else that you would like to share with me or Kayla? Now is the time to do it."

Thank God the direction of Evelyn's eyes shifted to Kayla. "I don't know where to start, Kayla, but I owe you an apology too. This is so hard for me to say, but as your best friend, I have betrayed you."

Kayla appeared out of it. All she did was move her head from side to side and bite her nails.

"I saw you at my house today. I went there to get Cedric to change his mind, but he didn't want to do it. He said that he didn't love me anymore, and I can't believe that he . . . just . . . does not love . . . me . . . anymore."

Kayla was in a daze. She looked straight ahead and didn't even turn to look at me or Evelyn. What in the hell was going on?

"What did you see going on between him and Evelyn? Did you see something?" I questioned. Evelyn sat still and waited for Kayla to respond.

Kayla rubbed her hands together and stood up. She paced the floor then stopped to squeeze her forehead. "I didn't see anything, but something is going on. I can feel it. You know how you have this . . . this eerie feeling inside that something is wrong. He said she was there for money, but I think there's more to it. I really do, but I just can't . . . I can't put my finger on it."

I was trying to pull this out of Kayla, especially since she was speaking as if Evelyn wasn't even there. "Well, put your finger on it and touch it. Open your eyes and see it. What are you feeling? Say it, Kayla, say it and don't lie to yourself anymore. Don't ignore what you know. Your gut has been telling you things, but you've been ignoring it. Rewind the tape and play those images in your head. Ask yourself: What do you see?"

Kayla closed her eyes and tears cascaded down her face. When she opened her eyes, she locked them on Evelyn. "I see Cedric and I see you, Evelyn. I've seen the way he looks at you and I've seen the way you smile at him. I saw him at your place one day," Kayla paused, sucked in a deep breath and released it. "And . . . and I saw your earrings and nasty panties in his car. I saw his account where he transferred thousands and thousands of dollars into your account and I . . . I smell the scent of my husband when I walk into your home. So the questions are: Are you fucking my husband, and if so, why didn't either of my best friends tell me what in the hell has been going on behind my back?"

I sat speechless, figuring that Kayla must have known about my betrayal as a friend too. Evelyn swallowed hard and sat with teary eyes. She blinked and scooted to the edge of the couch. "I'll answer your question, but for the record, you have never seen my nasty panties in Cedric's car. Those panties must have belonged to someone else. As I said before, I do owe you an apology—not for fucking your husband, but for allowing him to fuck me and use me to hurt you. For that, I am deeply sorry and I truly hope that you will one day forgive me for interfering in your marriage when I shouldn't have."

The room fell silent. Kayla glared at Evelyn without a blink and her fists quickly tightened. My breathing halted and I felt as if cement had been poured over me—I couldn't move. I could see beads of sweat dotting Evelyn's forehead and a slow tear slid down her face. The only thing that transformed the moment was the unique ring from Kayla's cell phone. The sound snapped her out of thoughts and she hurried to answer.

"I'll call you back, Jacoby," she said through gritted teeth. Then her face fell flat and her eyes widened. "What! Oh my God! I'll be there soon! Stay there!"

Kayla cut her eyes at Evelyn and me. She snatched her purse from the table and bolted to the door.

"What happened?" I yelled and jumped from my seat. "Please say something before you go."

Kayla didn't respond. The door flung open and slammed against the wall. A cool breeze blew in and I was left standing their counting the mistakes I had made while trying to refer to somebody as a best friend. I was in no position to call myself that and shame on me.

I hurried to call Jacoby, just to see if he would tell me why Kayla rushed out of there. When he answered his phone, I could hear loud cries over the phone.

"What's wrong, Jacoby?" I rushed to say. "Please tell me what's happening."

He gasped and released staggering cries. "My fa—fa-ther, Cedric, is dead. I think my mother killed him! She was so upset that she—she killed him!"

I thought about Kayla's unstable demeanor that was similar to Lexi's. My mouth opened wide and I dropped the phone, seeing it crash to the floor and break into pieces like our lives.

"What did he say?" Evelyn shouted out to me. "Why are you looking like that?"

I slowly turned my head to look at her. My mouth cracked open and I was now the one in a daze because I feared what Kayla had done.

"She—she killed him. Kayla killed Cedric."

I was shocked by Evelyn's reaction. She crossed her legs and shrugged her shoulders. "Like I've always said, too much pussy ain't good for you and a mad pussy is never a good thing. I'm deeply sorry for Kayla's loss. It's unfortunate."

I didn't bother to respond. I hurried out the door, hoping and praying that we would all recover from our tragedies.

Readers' Discussion Questions

1. Which one of the *BFF'S* can you relate to the most and why?

2. Do you think Kayla was wrong for not giving more money to her friends? Why or why not?

3. Do you believe that Trina is gay, or do you think she turned to women because of her past relationship?

4. Was it wise for Kayla to keep the secret about Arnez from Jacoby and Cedric?

5. Cedric blamed Kayla for turning him into the "monster" that he is. Do you believe that her lies made him betray her?

6. Could you ever forgive a friend for sleeping with your husband?

7. If you knew for a fact that one of your friends was sleeping with your other friend's husband, would you tell her? Why or why not?

8. What are your top requirements for someone to be considered a best friend?

9. Who do you believe shot Cedric?

10. Could you forgive the man in your life for giving you a sexually transmitted disease, even though you didn't enforce the use of condoms?

Notes